BADGER

SEALs of Steel, Book 1

Dale Mayer

Books in This Series:

Badger: SEALs of Steel, Book 1
Erick: SEALs of Steel, Book 2

D1089249

BADGER: SEALS OF STEEL, BOOK 1
Dale Mayer
Valley Publishing Ltd.

Copyright © 2018

This is a work of fiction. Names, characters, places, brands, media, and incidents are either the product of the author's imagination or are used fictitiously. Any resemblance to actual events, locales, or persons, living or dead, is entirely coincidental.

ISBN-13: 978-1-773360-74-4
Print Edition

About This Book

When an eight-man unit hit a landmine, all were badly injured but one died. The remaining seven aim to see his death avenged.

Badger knows those last-minute changes and the explosion were deliberate.

Kat is hooked on a man whose sole concern is retribution while she just wants happily-ever-after with him. Somehow she has to convince Badger love is preferable to answers gained only at the risk of dying to get them.

Sign up to be notified of all Dale's releases here!

http://dalemayer.com/category/blog/

Your Free Book Awaits!

KILL OR BE KILLED

Part of an elite SEAL team, Mason takes on the dangerous jobs no one else wants to do – or can do. When he's on a mission, he's focused and dedicated. When he's not, he plays as hard as he fights.

Until he meets a woman he can't have but can't forget. Software developer, Tesla lost her brother in combat and has no intention of getting close to someone else in the military. Determined to save other US soldiers from a similar fate, she's created a program that could save lives. But other countries know about the program, and they won't stop until they get it – and get her.

Time is running out ... For her ... For him ... For them ...

DOWNLOAD a *complimentary* copy of MASON? Just tell me where to send it!

http://dalemayer.com/sealsmason/

CHAPTER 1

KAT GREENWALD REACHED for her screwdriver and gently tightened the last adjustment on the state-of-the-art prosthetic leg in front of her. This was a new design, with a wider top, better balance, less material over all, but she hoped it was also stronger. Not the usual carbon fiber and polypropylene. Titanium had been added to the base, with a few other metals mixed in for strength. It still wouldn't be enough.

The man to wear this one was bent on destruction and refused to have the last surgery that would make his mobility that much better and his pain that much less. In her mind, she'd pegged the reason as he didn't care—or didn't think he'd live long enough to be bothered.

And she could do or say nothing to stop him from his chosen path. With a heavy sigh she stood and passed the prosthetic to Badger Horley.

Without a word, he took it, examined the changes she'd just made, gave a quick nod and put it on over the soft cotton wrapping on his stump. He stood and walked around the room.

Kat watched the huge man in front of her. He'd walked into her office and lab six months ago, desperate for her to put a leg on the end of his stump. But he hadn't been ready. The flesh on his stump hadn't healed enough. Any pressure caused a flare up and swelling, followed by infection. But he'd been adamant. He was determined to get on with his life.

She watched his face, not the leg, as he stepped around the room. The stump wasn't healed enough for her liking even now. He needed to stay off it for another three weeks. But that took her back to his stubbornness.

"You shouldn't stay on the leg more than ten to fifteen minutes at a time," she warned. "Otherwise you'll end up damaging the tissue next to the prosthetic, and the stump'll never heal. You know perfectly well your last infection damn near killed you."

He shot her a hard look but stayed silent.

She shrugged. "Or don't look after yourself. See if I care."

"It's not that bad."

"Right." She kept the rest of her thoughts to herself. When she came across somebody as driven and as angry as a badger, his namesake, she needed to stay the hell out of his way. The trouble was, she didn't want to stay out of his way. And the last thing she wanted was for him to head off on his personal vendetta. Revenge was a bitch. And it wouldn't keep him warm at night. There was always a price to pay when you went down that road.

Still, she had one more thing she could try.

She took the screwdriver back to her workbench and placed it in the case with the others. She turned and leaned against both her hands, so he couldn't see her white-knuckled grip on the bench. In a low voice she said, "Stone called."

He acted like he didn't hear her as he paced the room, testing his mobility, but she watched the muscle twitch in the corner of his jaw.

"He asked for your number."

He straightened and slowly turned to face her. "What did you tell him?"

"I told him that you are on a death mission. And likely to get yourself killed."

His gaze held a fury she had not seen before. She'd known it was inside, carefully hidden. It was evident in every line on that heavily muscled body as he twisted and turned, stretched and bent. Motions hard, sharp, jerky. When he put something down on a table, it landed with too much force. When he stood, it was too fast, chairs bouncing backward. Nothing in his life was relaxed and calm.

"You had no right."

Her eyebrows shot up. "No right to what? Answer his questions? I didn't overstep your HIPAA privacy rights. Stone and I have talked about prosthesis designs and shared findings long before you were my patient. He knew you were coming to see me but not from me. He called me, as your friend. And I'm not your therapist, but I have an opinion regardless. Plus you never said anything was top secret or superconfidential," she said in a hard tone. "You and I never really talk. I don't know where you live, who you're after or what asshole you're planning on putting six feet under. Stone asked me how you were doing, and I told him the truth."

Badger sucked his breath back and glared at her, his teeth clenched tight. "And what truth was that?"

"I said that you were hell-bent on killing yourself and wouldn't give your leg time to heal, and that I expected to hear you died from a septic infection within six weeks. That you were so focused on revenge that nothing else mattered, including having a future."

Badger snorted. "I have been looking after myself for a long time now. And my future does matter—at least once I deal with this issue. So no way would I let an infection like that take over my system."

She crossed her arms under her breasts. "Says you. But I've seen a man just as big and just as mean dropped for that exact reason. He became so focused on making sure he got back to what he considered a normal life that he forgot the warning signs. By the time he came in to me for an adjustment and an extra set of pads for comfort, he was already too far gone. But he wouldn't let anybody look at it. He wouldn't let anybody touch it. I'm the one who called the ambulance and had him shipped to the hospital. I never saw him again because he didn't make it. Four days later he was dead."

And that was no lie. It was one of the saddest truths she knew. She swore she'd never let that happen to another patient. But Badger was... well, Badger was past the point of her being able to do anything about his impending demise.

Not physically but emotionally, psychologically.

He stared at her, his gaze searching. "You've never mentioned that case before."

"Just like you, I have things I'd rather not talk about," she said smoothly. "And a patient I couldn't save—even though I'm the only one who acted in his best interests— makes it very difficult for me to speak about him."

"How long ago was this?"

"Four years. The kid was twenty-eight."

Badger's breath let out in a whoosh. He slid back inside himself, rethinking his actions. "My leg is not that bad."

"Your leg *is* bad. By the time it's *that* bad, it'll be way too late."

He rubbed his forehead. "I'll go home and take this off, and I'll wander around with crutches for a while. Will that make you happy?"

She shrugged. "It will make me *happier.* To see you stop your vendetta would make me the happiest."

He glared at her. "You take too much on yourself."

"I've been working with you for six months. I know dozens just like you. But you're the only one who'll ram his head against a brick wall in order to find the asshole who ruined your life."

He shook his head. "You don't know anything about it."

"Of course not. You don't talk. At least not to me. I highly doubt you've gone to a therapist either."

"I'm not that stubborn. It took a long time to deal with what happened."

"Adjustment always takes time. This wasn't an easy thing for you. But you've been flat on your back how many times since because you can't get that leg to heal? If you mess up now, *in any way*, you'll have major repercussions."

He raised both hands in frustration. "I know that. I'm not stupid."

"So then why is it I'm not allowed to tell Stone anything?"

Badger dropped his extremely muscled weight into the small chair she had set off to the side for visitors. She deliberately didn't keep it too comfortable. The last thing she wanted was for people to stay. They could come tell her whatever it was she needed to do to help them, and then they could leave. But she wasn't sure that chair, even for a short time, would sustain his mass. Badger came in the extra-large variety. At six-feet-six, 280 pounds, with both legs, he was a monster of a man. She'd never seen him lose his temper, but she knew it was big and hot and flashed fast. She could only hope he got over his anger just as easily.

"What did you do to my new leg?" he asked in an attempt to change the discussion.

"Changed the height of the cuff, ground down the edge and put a better joint in the knee. And, no, I haven't gotten to the point of building a weapon in there, but it's coming."

For the first time in a long time, a grin flashed. The same grin that had slammed into her heart six months ago when he had walked in her doorway for the first time.

"If and when you can do that, I really would like to be first on the list for that prototype."

She shook her head. "I'm not in the business of making weapons."

"You don't have to make them. You just have to find a way to hide them with easy access for us when we need them."

"I might have an idea or two on that. That's another reason Stone keeps calling. He's got a similar idea."

Badger nodded. "Stone's a good guy."

"That's what he said about you."

Badger dropped his gaze to the floor. "Did he say what he wanted?"

"I told you that he wanted your contact information. Something about having a lead."

Badger sucked in his breath, and his gaze locked on hers as if trying to reach into her soul and give her a shake. "Why didn't you say that in the beginning?"

She furrowed her brows and snapped, "I did."

He pinched the bridge of his nose and said, "No, you didn't. Not about him having a lead."

"It's not like he'll tell me anything about the business

between the two of you. But, if you were asking him for help, or if he was getting information for you, why the hell doesn't he have your contact information himself?"

"I lost my phone," Badger said quietly.

She studied his face for a long moment and shook her head. "Like hell."

Surprise hardened his gaze. "What do you mean?"

She shook her head again. "If you lost your phone, it's because you made it get lost. You're up to something. Before you leave town, make sure you pay my bill. If you're not coming back, I won't get paid."

He bounded to his feet, pulled out his wallet and handed her his credit card. "Then let's clear it up now."

She snatched the card from his hand and stalked to her desk, quickly taking care of the paperwork. The damn bill had nothing to do with this. She wanted something to shake him up. Jolt him out of his focus. When she turned and handed his card back to him, she said, "You have choices, you know."

He nodded, put away his credit card and walked to the front door before turning to look at her. "Sometimes those choices are made for us."

"No," she said, her tone soft, quiet, sad. "We still have to choose how we react. I don't know what devil is riding you, but I can guess. The thing is, if you keep going down that path, you'll never find the peace you want."

"Yeah, so now you're a shrink as well as a prosthetic de-signer?"

She shrugged, trying not to show the hurt deep inside. What had she expected? "I don't need a shrink's education to tell me that you're in a bad way. Everything you do is driven by anger and revenge. There is more to life than finding out who did this to you."

"It's not about who did this to *me*," he said, his tone hard, sober. "It's about who did this to my friends. Particularly Mouse, who right now would be dancing for joy to have a leg like mine. Only he can't because he's six feet under the ground." On that note he turned, walked through the front door and slammed it shut behind him.

BADGER WALKED OUT of the office, down the stairs and headed toward his truck. He was still riled on the inside but didn't dare show it. He had to control everything. She'd been wrong about one thing. He had been to a therapist. Several of them. He had been resistant to the idea, and it hadn't been an easy process. He kept hoping they would let him skate on the bigger issues. And finally, after quitting and trying again, several times over, he'd broken down enough to start discussing the real issues. But, even after that last therapist, Badger had walked out after her words wouldn't stop ringing through his head. She'd been adamant about him leaving behind the need for vengeance.

Bullshit.

Didn't anyone realize just how big this was? Didn't they realize his life had no meaning now that Mouse had died for nothing? He'd lost other friends in missions for the US Naval Services. Once a SEAL, always a SEAL. But none of them had hurt quite so bad as Mouse's death.

There'd been something about Mouse. His unit had all looked at Mouse like their own kid brother. The seven of them pre-Mouse had been tight, a team forged long before Mouse showed up. At first, they hadn't been sure about

Mouse joining them. But, when they saw the fuzzy-cheeked, scraggly looking kid, they'd shaken their heads and adopted him into the group. And he'd been the one who died. They'd all lost limbs, some more than one. But they were all alive.

Except for Mouse.

Badger knew accidents happened. He knew war happened, and there was never any good way to deal with such life-altering injuries. But he knew something had gone wrong that day. Their orders had changed at the very last minute. Somebody, somehow, had deliberately sent them in the direction of that buried mine. His gut told him so. For eighteen months his mind and brain had warred over the issue before finally landing on the same side as his gut. And that breach of ethics was inexcusable. He just had to find out how and who.

Then maybe he could move forward.

No way could he move forward if he didn't make that asshole pay. He just didn't know how yet. Hell, he didn't know who yet either.

Sometimes he woke up in the middle of the night with his fists clenched, his body locked in agony—his mind reliving over and over again how he lay in the hot sand, hearing his friends crying out beside him. But two years ago, the way he was positioned, all he could see was Mouse crumpled beside him. That had been the day from hell.

When he struggled to inspect his own body, he found his leg gone, his gut wrenched opened, and his arm and back filled with shrapnel. He'd managed to get a call out for help, then dragged himself to Erick's side, grabbing his hand and telling him to hold on. He didn't remember much after that. He lost consciousness and woke up in the military hospital just before they put him under the knife. He remembered crying out to the doc to save Mouse first, and the doc slapping a mask over his face and telling him to go to sleep. He had slept but not by choice.

And when he woke up, his worst nightmare had come true. The others tried to tell him to ease back, and he knew they all felt the loss as keenly as he did. But, for some reason, he couldn't get over it. He hoped they had. He stayed in contact with all of them, but he wasn't sure any of them felt this same need that he did for vengeance. He knew it was twisting him up, poisoning his life, stopping him from having a future, like everybody around him urged him to have. But how did he move forward when he knew somebody had deliberately thrown him and his team into this nightmare? And was probably sitting back and laughing about it.

He shook his head, unlocked his truck door and hopped in. That movement pulled a muscle in his back. He sat there, gasping for a long moment. Just as he put the keys in the ignition, his phone rang. He pulled out his cell, saw the name on the screen and smiled. "Well, I guess she handed you my contact information after all. Stone, what's up?"

"Not much. You?" Stone's voice was hard, determined, and yet there was a hint of caution. As if he was determining where the hell Badger was on this path called life.

Badger smiled. "I'm sitting outside Kat's office. She made some changes on my prosthetic. I'm hoping this time it won't sore my leg up quite so bad."

"You know it needs time to heal. Give your leg a break before you wear the prosthetic again. Not everybody has a clean amputation. They try, but some tendons and muscles don't grow back the way they're supposed to."

"Isn't that the truth? Apparently I had nothing but hamburger left. Trouble is, every time I put any weight on it, it still feels that way," he growled.

"I know the feeling."

Badger leaned back to stare out the window. That was the thing about Stone. He was in the same boat Badger was in. But he had been there a little longer. He'd had time to heal. Time to adjust. Badger was still dealing with the original fallout. "Why'd you call, man?"

"Got a little bit of intel."

"Yeah, on what?" He turned on the engine while he waited for Stone to spell it out.

"On a directive that sent you in a certain direction that morning."

Instantly his hand turned the key to shut off the engine. The silence filtered around him like some kind of shock wave. "What directive?" he asked, his voice quiet. It had to be quiet because he wanted to reach through the phone and shake Stone, clasp his hands around the big man's neck and squeeze for taking so long to give him the answers Badger was so desperate to receive.

"Not a ton of information yet, just a line."

"Tell me," Badger barked.

"The plans were changed that morning, but you didn't hear that from me."

"From what plan to what plan?" Badger asked. Why would the directives have been changed? "How good is your intel?"

"It's good. It's just that it's been two years. According to the intel, somebody is finally talking. But he was at a bar, drunk. So I don't know how good it is."

"You just said it's good." Inside Badger could feel hope

starting to splinter. Over the last couple years, he'd heard lots. People pointed in many directions. It always came down to the fact *it was an official decision. It was an accident. Nobody knew about the land mine. Things like that happened in war.* He understood that. But, at the same time, he'd wondered. They'd been redirected, on a different route. Why?

Had somebody known that land mine was on that road? The road they were instructed to take had been changed. Was it just a shitty coincidence, or was somebody really sabotaging an entire unit? And, if that was the case, why?

He'd racked his brain over the last two years for the same damn reason. Not one of his team knew anything worth getting killed over. Everybody knew the same shit. They hadn't been on any particular mission in the weeks prior. They hadn't been hunting down any one asshole over any other asshole. The world was full of them. When they were working in Afghanistan, there were more than a few. But they hadn't been after any leaders on that particular day. It had just been a shitty accident, according to the report. But inside Badger knew it was more than that. He just hadn't been able to prove it.

"You still there?"

"Yeah, I'm still here. Whatever you've got, shoot it to me in an email, will you?"

"Will do." Stone hesitated for a moment, then added, "And give that damn leg a rest, will you? When the time does come to move, you won't be ready if it isn't." And he hung up.

Badger snorted, tossed his phone on the seat beside him, turned the engine back on and pulled out into traffic.

Stone was right about one thing. The leg wasn't any

good as it was right now. He needed to get off it and let it heal a bit more. But he sure as hell hated to. He'd put out a ton of money trying to get the information he needed. And, so far, there'd been nothing. All coming back negative. *Somebody—somewhere—*had to know something. His worst nightmare was to continue searching for answers only to find out there really weren't any, and it was truly a shitty accident. If he could believe that himself, then maybe he could learn to live with it and move forward.

There were other things to want in life. At one point in time, he'd wanted a family. Now? Well, hell. A steady girlfriend would be a step up.

His mind fleetingly went to Kat. The only woman to interest him in years. She was one hell of a woman. Smart, intelligent, capable, direct. He liked them direct. That she was missing a leg wasn't something he held against her. And, if nothing else, it made her more sympathetic to him. And him to her.

The trouble was, he didn't want sympathy. He wanted to be the dashing hero who swept her off her feet and carried her into the wild blue yonder. But that wouldn't happen. He was doing weight training again. Part of the reason why his stump had bombed out. Although Kat didn't weigh much, he certainly wasn't up to doing that kind of coordinated effort.

He drove down the main road for another couple miles, then took a right, thinking about what Stone had said. Had he deliberately held back a little bit? Badger knew Stone. They were the same type of guy. But Stone had somehow gotten past his anger. His personality was more laid back. But then again, Stone losing his leg had been part of an active mission. Not like Badger, driving over a land mine when your unit was potentially not where it was supposed to be in the first place, doing some recon work.

He shook his head. "I've got to get out of this endless loop."

It took another ten minutes to get home. Badger opened the truck door, stepped down, landed a bit hard on the sore leg, swore a blue streak and slammed the truck door shut. Dotty, an aging coonhound, greeted him with her usual loving barks and yelps. He'd found her on the side of the road where she'd been shot by her previous owner. He'd picked her up, plucked out the bullet himself, got her back onto her feet and had been looking after her ever since. Or was it really that she looked after him? They were both lost and wounded dogs.

She was good people, and he was doing the best he could to be good people to her. They'd both learned some tough lessons, and the bottom line was, people couldn't be trusted. Now if only he could find out who the hell had betrayed him and his team.

Just as he walked in and pulled a cold beer from the fridge, his phone rang. He pulled it from his pocket. "Kat, what's up?"

"You left some of your gear here," she said. "That's not like you."

He swore softly. "What the hell did I leave?"

"The original pieces on your leg that you'll need for spare parts. And your multitool that you brought out to show me how you've been trying to fix the one joint. When I told you to put that piece of crap away, you didn't. You just set it down."

"I won't need either of those for the next couple days. I'll stop by when I head back into town next."

"Good enough."

He thought she'd hung up, but he heard her swear. "What's up?"

"Nothing," she said quietly. "I'll see you in a few days." Then she did hang up.

He stared at the phone in his hand and wondered. Something about her voice had been odd before she ended the call. What the hell was wrong?

He placed his phone in his pants pocket, snagged his beer and headed out on the porch. Whatever the hell was wrong, it would be a long cold day before she told him. He couldn't afford to be sidetracked, even by the very sexy Kat. Unfortunately.

Sitting on the wooden chair he kept on the porch, yet still unsettled, cold beer in hand, his laptop balanced on his thighs, he brought up his email program and waited for Stone's email to land in his inbox. He clicked it open as soon as it had and read the short message. He pulled out his phone, quickly dialing Stone. "Why the hell didn't you tell me that you had a name?"

"You didn't give me much chance." Stone's tone held a bit of humor. "I figured you'd get back to me when you read it."

"I want to talk to this guy," he said.

"Good luck with that. He wasn't very talkative to anyone apparently."

"Do you have any contact information?" Badger reread the email but still didn't get anything more from it. "Your email is a little short on substance."

Stone chuckled. "I don't want you going off half-cocked and getting yourself blown up again."

"Why not? The first time was so much fun."

Stone's voice dropped all hilarity when he said, "This could be bad. *You* know that."

"I know. It's not just about me. There are seven of us. We're all in various states of getting back on our feet. I haven't spoken to them about this, but, now that I have a lead, I know they will want to know who's behind this. It's up to us to find the asshole who did this."

"Then let us help. While you know a lot of men still active in the units, there's our team out here."

"You guys are more of a unit now than you ever were." Badger thought about Levi and the crew he'd pulled together that made up the company of Legendary Security. "But it's bad enough that some of us will risk our lives and whatever is left of our pensions and medical support to do this. We don't want anybody else to get hurt."

"Bullshit." Stone gave a half snort. "You can pull that line on somebody else. Not with us. You'll need help. You'll need weapons. You'll need intel. We've got eyes in the sky, and we've got people all over the world. You know that."

Badger pinched the bridge of his nose. He knew he was doing way too much lately. It went along with the frustration in his life. "Some of that might be helpful, but, if it ever comes back that you civilians have stepped into naval matters to make this happen, you know it won't go well for Levi or anyone else. And that's not good."

"And you know that, if Levi gives you a hand, Mason will want to do what he can too."

"Oh, hell no. He's still active duty. That'll be treason if he gets caught."

"*Treason?*" Stone's voice took on a thoughtful, pensive tone. "*Treason* if we find the asshole who blew up our own units? Somehow I don't think that's the definition of *treason*.

Will Mason get official clearance to help? I doubt it. But that doesn't mean he won't cross the line and do what's right. You know Mason is all about doing what's right. He's a man of honor."

"He is that." Badger couldn't argue that point. They were all the same breed. After he ended the call, Badger got up and looked across the yard. The pool twinkled in the light. He ignored it. His mind was twisting and turning on this tidbit of information. He finished his beer, walked back inside to the fridge and grabbed a second one. Just as he popped the top, he heard the *ding* on his laptop, telling him another email had come in.

He walked around the desk to check it. Another one from Stone. No wording, just a phone number. Badger raised his eyebrows, pulled out his cell phone again and dialed the number. Instantly a message on the other end of the line swept through. *A voice almost recognizable.*

But not quite. He frowned as he listened to the standard *I'm not here but please leave a message at the sound of the beep.* Instead he hung up and dropped the phone on the desk. The least Stone could have done was say a little bit more about who the number belonged to. And maybe that was the trick. Stone had a phone number but no names. Intel, when it came, was often only a portion of what they needed. Badger sat down and searched a site for the phone number but came up with nothing.

His phone rang a few minutes later. He picked it up and frowned when he saw the same number ID on the display dial. "Hello?"

"You called me." The voice was hard, curt.

"I did. Looking for information on a change of orders from two years ago." He heard the sucked-in breath of the man on the other end and realized this asshole knew something. "I pay for solid information," he said calmly.

"How much?"

Badger leaned back in the chair and thought about this turn of events. "It depends on how good it is."

"It's hard to say. Two years is a long time ago."

"Do you know something, or don't you?"

"I know the order was changed."

"I know it was changed too. But by who and why?"

"A phone call came in, saying the original route was bad, and to make a last-minute change."

Badger leaned forward and then stood. "Who made that phone call?"

"I don't know. It came through secure lines. It had to be somebody out in the field that morning."

"Was the information checked and confirmed?"

"There was no time. In order to save the men out in the field, the change of direction was done immediately."

Badger swore softly under his breath. He could see that happening. Any intel had to be accepted or rejected on the fly. Information was fluid. They would pick up a tidbit here and a tidbit there. But they had to be prepared to act. They'd been given their instructions; then they'd been given a new set on the way. It hadn't been anything they had questioned. That was why they'd taken the change of direction. "No way to find out who that phone call came from?"

"Not with the security level I have. Or at the level anybody I know has."

"Any suspicions?"

The man took a deep breath. "Yeah. From inside the truck that blew up."

And he hung up.

CHAPTER 2

FOR THE REST of that afternoon, Kat found herself staring off into space, caught on the enigma that was Badger. He cared about her but couldn't let himself follow up. He might even be deliberately blocking his feelings.

He couldn't afford to let anything interfere with his revenge plan.

She didn't know all the details of the originating event, but this anger had been evident every time she'd seen him. She had also seen several of his navy friends from the same unit. She'd picked up little bits and pieces from each of them. The accident had been bad—not one of the eight-man team had escaped unscathed. She'd understood it *was* an accident. However, they had been in a war-torn country, driving in military vehicles while on active duty. Were there such things as accidents then?

She dropped the folder she'd been working on to the stack at her side. Jim would come and retrieve them and refile at the end of the day. She was overwhelmed with work right now and would once again be taking her designs home to work on there as well. Most of her patients were simple cases, but a few, like Badger, required specialized designs. He'd lost his leg at midthigh and needed more muscle built up at the end for padding against the prosthetic cup. But he didn't want more surgery.

In the back of her mind she worried he didn't figure to be around long enough to make it worthwhile.

He didn't give a damn about that either.

And that hurt. She wanted to be enough for him to change his mind. To care enough to come back to her. She didn't have any idealistic views of what a relationship with this man would entail. He'd never been an easy patient. The good news was, she'd already seen him at his worst. Nothing like a disgruntled patient to show her the man's dark side. But that was only a prelude to the volcanic force being held back inside.

Jim's head popped around the corner. "The next patient just called. He's had a breakdown and is stuck on the side of the road. He wants to reschedule for next week."

She nodded. "That's fine. Any other patients this afternoon?" She flipped through her daily paper calendar atop her desk. A canceled appointment in many ways was a gift.

"No, you're done now." He gave her a wide grin and a thumbs-up. "But don't appear too happy. You're several prototypes behind."

She groaned. "I know. Sadly. Close my door. No disturbances for the rest of the afternoon."

He closed the door quietly. She returned to the stacks of files on her desk. Where to start? For the next two hours she buried her head in Stacking's file. He needed a better connection for his forearm. The car accident took off his arm at an angle, and the surgeon at the time had closed up the arm with the intent of keeping the man alive. The subsequent reconstructive surgery had taken a couple years, and she still didn't have much to work with.

When she lifted her head and looked around later, she found complete silence. No noise even came from the main office. She stood and stretched. Had Jim left?

Moving slowly and breathing deeply, she walked to her office door and opened it. The lights and computer were off in the main office. She glanced at the wall clock. It was after five.

She rotated her neck to loosen the kinks. She had a habit of getting so involved that she lost track of everything else. Like today. She walked to the window, still adjusting to pull her out of her intense work mode. The late-afternoon sun was starting to fall, but it would be light for hours yet. Her gaze landed on a man leaning against a tree on the far side of the street. He was on his cell phone.

Just like so many, he appeared to be unaware of what was going on around him. The digital world dominated every corner of society. It was a constant surprise to her, but still she was no better, having just now spent hours on the computer, researching. The world had changed.

As she moved to the side of the window she caught a shift in the man's head movement.

Suspicious, but not knowing why, she deliberately stepped back out of sight.

The stranger glanced around, then looked up to study her window. Unnerved, she watched until he walked toward the street corner, pocketing his phone. Feeling better, she returned to her computer. She had a few things to finish up; then she'd head home.

As she set her security alarm, she once again had a weird feeling, setting the hairs on the back of her neck upright. She had no idea why she felt so unnerved.

Except it was Tuesday.

And that meant another letter would arrive tomorrow.

They always came on a Wednesday.

THAT NIGHT WAS one of the worst. Badger tossed and turned, woke up in a cold sweat, dropped back into sleep again, only to be blown up time and time again as his mind relived the horror of what he'd been through. Only now was the added element of somebody making a phone call. He tried to cast his mind back to that time, but he'd been riding shotgun in the front of the vehicle. He couldn't tell who might have been sending a text or making a phone call behind him. They'd been in good spirits; the day was hot, sunny, with everyone in a good mood and good health.

There was no sense of betrayal or gut warning about what was ahead of them. Shit happened. But they had no idea they were about to become part of the manure pile themselves. Nothing indicated they were being hunted or under attack in any way. They'd been driving for two hours. They'd stopped once for water and just to take a look around the area. They'd found nothing.

It was a simple recon trip to a village a few miles farther past the accident site.

After all this time, Badger couldn't even remember the conversations they'd been engaged in beforehand. But he knew they'd been laughing and joking—yet keeping steady eyes on all things around them as they drove forward. Nothing came to mind as out of the ordinary. It made him sick to his stomach to think the call came from somebody inside the truck. It was horrible to look at your friends suspiciously and wonder if they'd betrayed you. He shook his head. "No way in hell."

Badger rose from the bed, grabbed his crutches and headed to the glass door to the small balcony, opened the curtains and stared out at the New Mexico desert beyond his street. There was nobody to look back. They would have gotten an eyeful if they had. He opened the glass door and stepped out, waiting for the slightly cooler night air to waft over his heated body.

His current life barely resembled his previous world. Not his family, not his home, not his body, not his lifestyle, not his employment. None of it. He used to have a career with the navy. He used to have a long-term girlfriend. He'd expected to get married and to settle down. Even had the house for them all planned out in the back of his head. But, like his physical body, everything else had blown up. And he'd lost it all. His girlfriend hadn't wanted to be part of his recovery process. And when she had realized he'd lost a leg, torn the muscles in his back and would never be quite the same big strong strapping healthy male she had spent two years with—pre-accident—she'd walked.

And he'd moved home, needing his mother's care.

At the time he'd been so angry and so deep in depression. His girlfriend leaving was just one more door slammed in his face. One more dart in his heart. For a long time, he wanted to commit suicide, contemplated it, worked out in his mind what would be a good way to do it. But in the VA hospital, he saw so many other men worse off than him that he'd been ashamed of himself.

And then Stone had walked in, taken one look at him and grinned. Just something about that vibrant healthy fully recovered man in front of him—standing on a pretty incredible prosthetic—made Badger realize that, although he was broken and down at the time, he didn't have to stay that way. That life offered so much more.

Back then Stone had reached out a hand and had

helped, and Badger realized the best thing he'd ever done was reach back.

Stone had wanted Badger to come and work for Levi, but that hadn't been Badger's thing.

In many ways Badger was afraid he didn't have anything left to give. Part of the drive pushing his recovery had been his need for answers. He was still so tied up in knots over what had happened, so driven by the need to find out if something ... *wrong* had gone on, that he was useless to anybody else until he addressed that issue.

He pivoted on his crutches, turned his back to the cool outside breeze, waiting for the sweat to dry on his skin. He stared at the tumbled bed, seeing the bedcovers twisted up, as if he'd been in the middle of a fight, and realized it would be hard to catch any more sleep tonight.

He wondered how Stone had reacted to the newest information Badger had gotten.

He checked his clock on the bedside table and saw it was only three in the morning. He grabbed his boxers and a pair of shorts, threw on a muscle shirt, his prosthetic, only wincing slightly, and walked out the front door, heading for his sneakers. Dotty met him at the door. When his foot hit the top step, he took off, the dog running happily at his side.

Being a coonhound, she could run like the wind. Aged, she might be, but she wasn't done for. And he wasn't done for either.

He headed for the open area beside his place, his feet pounding the flat terrain, avoiding the worst of the rocks in the half-light, every once in a while coming down unsteadily and having to correct his balance and posture before he was sent flying. If nothing else, he would give the new prosthetic a workout.

And likely sore his leg up further. But some demons couldn't be exorcised any other way.

That thought sent his mind back to Kat. He hadn't told her what he was up to, but she'd known. Somehow she'd known. She was also very intuitive and experienced with trauma patients. It had been Kat who suggested he just stop doing too much—as if she understood the devil that rode him. And, instead of looking for a nice peaceful ride, the devil sought a wild bucking bronco moment.

Unfortunately the devil seemed to have found that with Badger.

Maybe his obsession wasn't any surprise, given what he'd been through. He was lucky he was only missing a leg. Yet he wasn't done with his rehab. He needed another surgery. The circulation was impaired and needed to be improved. But he'd balked at it. The doctors had said he'd end up with permanent damage if he didn't have this next surgery. Plus it would give him more tissue in his stump. He'd lost the leg pretty damn high up. He didn't have much of a stump, like Stone. And, no, Badger hadn't adjusted as well as Stone had. Badger wasn't sure he ever would. His mind was consumed with the latest doctor's words as Badger ran and ran and ran. *The nervous system at the stump wasn't doing as well as it should. The circulatory system was compromised, and Badger was in danger of losing more of his leg,* which meant no prosthetic. And that meant crutches and possibly a wheel-chair.

The sweat rolled down his back as he looped his way around, finally heading home again. He looked down at Dotty. She was loping in a steady pace at his side. Happy to go where he went. Happy to just be.

He wondered why he couldn't find that same sense of

satisfaction.

When he finally walked back the last hundred yards to his place, he could feel his heart calming down. Yet, instead of relaxing, his muscles were tensing. A hot shower would help. Or a swim but the heat would be better. And he was too tired to swim. The land mine had damaged the muscles in his back. The scar tissue was thick and rigid, and he'd spent hours in the gym, trying to build up some of the missing muscle. But the whole left side of his upper and lower back was pretty ugly looking. He didn't give a damn what it looked like, but he needed to know the muscle was there when he reached for it. That he had the power he needed when he had to pull on them. And, at the moment, it still wasn't that good. But then some things would just never be perfect. Humpty Dumpty might be put back together again, but nobody ever said he was put back together again *well*.

Badger walked inside, shed his clothes and his prosthetic, and hopped in the shower once the water got hot enough. When he finally stepped from the shower, he slipped on his prosthetic and walked over to the kitchen to put some heat under his coffee maker. It was five o'clock now.

He opened and turned on his laptop. Instantly it pinged with an email. He sat down to see another one from Stone. *We're here for you. Make the right call.* Badger snorted and stood, headed to the cupboard, grabbed a clean coffee cup and poured himself some of the brew, even though it was still dripping. He ignored the splash as the drops of coffee hit the burner beneath.

Stone might want Badger to make the right call on this new info, but, at the moment, he couldn't make any call. He didn't know what the next step was. The thought of researching and investigating any of the men in that vehicle that day—his friends—made him sick to his stomach and turned the inside of his mouth bitter. How could he find out the truth? Two other trucks had been out with his unit. In his mind he wanted it to be somebody from one of those vehicles. He did have a list of the men in the other vehicles and knew some of them personally but not all of them.

It was possible one of those men had put in the call. Had they done it deliberately, knowing what the outcome would be? Or had that been a case of they'd received bad intel too?

It was hard to wait for the coffee to cool enough to drink.

He was physically tired, but his mind was alive, alert, moving at a rapid speed, only it was going in circles. Finally he returned to the laptop, sat down and emailed Stone an update. Badger hadn't had time to finish his cup of coffee when the phone rang.

"What will you do about it?"

Badger smiled. "I don't know yet. We were meeting up at a village. There were three vehicles involved. Two were aging Humvees carrying four men each. My unit was in a light tactical vehicle—four men inside and four men riding in the back. We were the only vehicle blown up."

"You think the directive came from one of the other two trucks?"

"It's much easier to think that than to consider it came from one of my own men."

Stone whistled. "That wouldn't make any sense if it came from one of your guys. That would be a suicide mission."

"Mouse is the only one who died. And he's the last one who wanted to commit suicide."

Stone hesitated, then asked, "Are you sure about the other six?"

"As sure as I can be. I worked with those men for years. Mouse was the only newbie."

"Any idea on the financial situation of any of them? Anybody truly suicidal? Anybody recently broken up? Anything that would suggest a land mine was a possible end?"

"Hell no." Badger got up to refill his coffee cup. "All of us are broken. Not one of us walked out without severe injuries."

"In suicide attempts that often happens. People jump off a bridge. But they don't quite kill themselves. They just break their neck instead, and they get to spend the rest of their life, lying on a bed, being spoon-fed, with a catheter up their ass."

"Sounds horrible. And I still don't think it's any one of my guys."

"You know you need to talk to them about it." Stone's voice was low, confident.

"I spent the last two years contemplating this. It never occurred to me the phone call came from one of us."

"You guys were always close. And I know what that's like because that's how we were too."

"I know. I want an answer, and I want an easy answer. I don't want all the shit that just keeps getting in the way."

"But the problem is, you want to find an answer—even if there isn't one."

"That still sucks."

"But you have to talk to your unit. That's where you start. Tell them what bit of intel has popped up to see if anyone knows the other men. As you and I both know, a shitty order starts with shitty intel."

Badger hung up, walked back to his French doors and stared outside. It was too early to call anyone else. He sat down, wincing at the sore on his leg. He pulled off the prosthetic and stared at the bloody swelling. "Shit."

He grabbed the crutches that were always close by and hobbled over to the medicine cabinet. There he pulled out disinfectant and dabbed the side of his stump. It was pretty easy to have a small problem morph into a big one. He put several more bandages on.

Back at the table he picked up the prosthetic and took a careful look. Kat had built up the inside with extra padding. But it wasn't enough. His skin was so sore and raw still. He needed time to build it up, but of course he hadn't thought about that when he took off for a flat-out run—nor had he cared as he was so caught up with his demons.

Then he wasn't in a position to get picky. He was mobile, and that was more than he thought to ever be.

It just wasn't quite enough.

CHAPTER 3

THAT MORNING KAT woke up late. She hopped out of bed, forgot about coffee or breakfast, and drove straight to the office. She had patients all morning. By the time she had her first break, and her fifth cup of coffee, she turned to find somebody she knew well standing in front of her. She glanced at Badger with a frown as he walked toward her. His stride listed heavily to the side, but he was trying to hide it—and failing. As soon as he made it inside her office, she snapped, "What the hell did you do to yourself now?"

His glared deepened. "How do you know I did anything?"

"Because you're limping."

He glared at her harder. "I went running. And I forgot."

"You forgot what?"

"I forgot I was supposed to take it easy."

"You forgot?" She stared at him, her jaw slowly dropping. "Are you nuts?" She motioned for him to sit down. "Let me take a look."

He sat down, a bit too forcefully.

Kat rarely allowed anybody to give her a hard time while in the chair. Her patients were often big strong men who could've swatted her like a fly across the room. But she had a skill they all needed. Or, if they would at least take care of themselves, they could put her skill to use. When she dealt with somebody like Badger, she was lucky if she was allowed to help at all. She carefully removed the prosthetic, took one look at the bandage underneath, shook her head and ripped it off.

He gave a sharp cry. "What the hell was that for?"

"I can't fix what I can't see." She took a long, careful look at the swollen tissue and the location in reference to the prosthetic. Then she looked at the metal, but nothing was wrong there. She frowned, put the prosthetic back on with a new bandage over the top of the rubbed area. "Stand up and walk toward me."

He did as told and walked toward her carefully.

She held up her hand to stop him, then dropped to her knees with a screwdriver and her calipers. "You've thrown the ankle joint off," she muttered to herself as she took some measurements, made him do several test passes. Finally she had it back in her hands again and adjusted the ball joint ever-so-slightly. "This should fix that problem. You'll get your new prosthetic as soon as I can get the parts delivered." She glanced up at him. "What sent you out running so hard you had to hurt yourself?"

He gave her a flat stare.

She sighed. "Nightmares by any chance?"

Instead of being belligerent or saying something snappy, he just shrugged.

She felt her insides soften. "I'm grateful to not have that problem. I understand time does help them diminish."

He nodded. "I know. That doesn't make it any easier."

"True enough. Did you talk to Stone?" she asked abruptly. She watched his head slowly go up and down, and her heart sank. "Did you get a lead?"

He quirked an eyebrow at her and continued the same

movement, his gaze questioning.

She'd always found it hard to read him. He hid behind a wave of black anger. It was hard to see inside to the heart of him. "You're good to go. Of course it would be a whole lot better if you'd use crutches for several weeks. Bed rest would be best."

"I'll go to bed if you go too," he said in a mocking tone.

She wondered what he'd do if she ever took him up on it. It would be sex for the sake of sex because he didn't give a damn about anyone. She just waved her hand at him. "You say that to all the girls."

"How much, Doc?"

She shook her head. "This one's on me. Please, would you go back to your crutches and give that leg time to heal?"

"No, not going to happen. I'm likely to be heading overseas pretty quick."

She froze, shoved her hands deep in her pockets to hide her fingers clenching into fists. "Why?"

He gave her a lopsided smile, one that tugged at her heart. "The lead from Stone. Might need to chase down some people, just to talk to them."

In a smooth tone she said, "Have fun." And she walked back to her desk. If she sat down a little too hard, nobody could blame her surely.

"Never want to pull any punches do you, Doc? Can't wait to see the back of me." He gave her a jaunty wave, grabbed his stuff he'd left behind last time and walked out.

She wondered at their constant banter. Always dancing back and forth, never quite critical, never quite sexual. But it was always there underneath. She wondered if he had a hard time with the fact that she was missing a leg. She had no problem with him missing a leg. But that didn't mean the perfect man who thought he should be the big macho dude wasn't looking for the perfect woman. She'd spent enough years dealing with the problem of believing she was less than whole herself. She didn't need her boyfriend doing it too.

Of course she'd been missing a leg for most of her life— amputated when she was only four years old. It had stopped growing soon after birth. She was long used to this reality. She'd also had several long-term relationships. She'd only chosen men who understood. Anybody who was looking for a model-perfect woman at his side be damned. She was all woman—and that meant good days and bad days. Not just phony perfection.

She sat down, brought up her email and sent a message. *He's gone again. Leg is suffering. Inflammation is worse. Puffiness hard to fit the prosthetic. He won't slow down, won't stay off the leg to heal.* She hit Send in frustration, without giving it a thought. When her phone rang a few minutes later, she picked it up and answered in a distracted voice. "Hello?"

"Isn't there any way to take the leg away from him for a while?" the caller asked in exasperation.

She chuckled. "If you can't keep your old buddy in check, how do you expect me to?"

"Bat your eyelashes at him, shake your hips, do something. Badger's very susceptible to the female form," Erick joked.

She shook her head, realizing, of course, he couldn't see it, then she said, "Not going to happen."

"Still carrying a torch for him?"

She froze. With a fake laugh she said, "Don't know what you're talking about."

She knew she'd failed to convince him when he just

chuckled that deep knowing chuckle. Erick had been injured at the same time as Badger. But Erick came to see her sooner, and he had healed, inside and out, faster. And he kept talking about how worried he was about one of the guys— Badger.

As a matter of fact, she'd seen files on all seven of the members of that same unit. But then she was one of the top prosthetic designers in the world, which meant a lot of injured men and women came to her, stationed here in New Mexico. At least for initial testing. And, once one of the men had come, it seemed natural for them to recommend her to the others. Funny, all of the guys she saw in Badger's unit were all worried over Badger's mental and physical state.

And not without reason.

Erick said, "Did you get those runner blades in yet?"

"Yours are here."

"Great. Maybe I'll pop round this afternoon."

"Do that." She hesitated, then added, "He got a lead on something."

Silence.

She winced. "I wouldn't normally say anything. But I kind of feel like I'm betraying him if I do and you if I don't."

"A lead on what?"

"On what happened. Stone gave him something. I don't know."

"Stone told you that?"

She relayed the turn of events that had her caught in the middle.

"Interesting. I think I might drive past Badger's place today. Sounds like the man needs a friend."

"He looked like he'd taken a blow. As if something he hadn't quite expected had happened."

"Very interesting," he said in a quiet voice. "I'll definitely run by his place today then." And he hung up.

Not knowing if she'd done the right thing, she put the phone down beside her and got back to work. For every patient she had, there was a ton of paperwork to maintain. She kept medical records, not to mention fitness reports and detailed dimensions of every adjustment she made. By the time she was done, she was ready for her next patient.

When she looked up, it was now two o'clock in the afternoon, the lunch hour long gone. She leaned back and groaned, brushing the flyaway blond hair off her forehead.

Jim popped his head around the corner and grinned at her. "You always overwork yourself. If you would leave the work at the office, … instead of taking it home at night …"

"I have too much on my plate for that," she said irritably. "Maybe I should cut back on my appointment schedule."

"And then somebody gives you a sob story, and you fit them in," he said in a good-natured tone.

She rolled her eyes at him. But he was right. She looked around her office, but she'd run out of her house this morning a bit late and hadn't packed lunch.

Just then Jim stepped toward her with a plate in hand. His grin brightened when he saw her eyes light up.

She shook her head and reached out. "Dear God, I hope that's for me."

He chuckled. "It was actually my lunch," he said magnanimously, "but I made two sandwiches. So here, have one."

She took the plate gratefully, picked up half a sandwich and bit in. It was delicious. She chewed for a long moment and shook her head. "I think you're the only person I know who puts jam on a sandwich with cheese, meat, onions, pickles, lettuce ..." She eyed the sandwich as she named off a few other things.

"If you don't like it ..."

She nudged the plate closer toward her. "I didn't say I didn't like it. I just never had a meat sandwich with jam in it before."

He shot her a look. "You were raised with PB and J. What's not to like about it in this sandwich? It's my fave."

She nodded. "Of course it is."

But before he could make any comment, she took another big bite. It didn't matter that it was odd or different. It was food, and right now she was starving and needed it. Bonus that it was seriously tasty. She still had a long afternoon to get through. And she wouldn't make it if she didn't start taking care of herself. But somewhere in the last month or two, when she realized just how much she was starting to care about Badger, she had stopped sleeping. And that was not a good thing.

Lying in bed thinking about the damn man—who was stubborn, obnoxious, cranky and cantankerous half the time—was not good for her own soul. On the other hand, she hadn't had a date in a long time. Maybe it was just sexual frustration. Maybe she really should call up an old friend and go for a date or two ...

She shook her head. That so wasn't her style.

She might have done that when she was younger, but she'd passed that stage at least a decade ago. Now at thirty-three she was looking for something a whole lot more than a one-night stand. She loved sex. It was fun. It was easy. It made her feel good. But only with the right man. She wasn't into sex with strangers.

Now Badger was a whole different story. He wasn't a stranger, though she wasn't sure she'd call him a friend either. But sparks flew when they were together, even if they avoided bringing up the topic. She'd been nice; she'd been patient, but she was getting pretty tired of both. If she could just run into him somewhere, she'd probably take him to bed, have those pants off him and him flat on his back before he ever knew what hit him. Trouble was, she was always stuck in the office, and he was always hiding away in his own place. And, so far, the two of them hadn't crossed paths anywhere else.

When she put the last of the sandwich in her mouth, she shifted the plate out of her way as Jim returned with the mail. She marveled that people still sent paper mail. She much preferred email and digital copies. She shook her head. "In this day and age, physical mail shouldn't be a thing."

He laughed. "That's quite true."

She quickly sorted through it. He had opened the bulk of it, but a couple looked more personal. She frowned, grabbed the letter opener and slid one of the envelopes open. She pulled out a letter from a former patient. He was just giving her an update and had sent her some pictures.

She took a look and smiled. "This one is from Gordon. He's doing fantastic," she exclaimed, studying the photos.

She got up, and, with stickpins in one hand and photos in the other, pinned them to her big wallboard. She loved it when her patients sent her photos. It was always nice to keep in touch with them too. Gordon was a good guy. He'd married last year, and she wished nothing but the best for him. She tucked his letter away into a personal folder and tossed the envelope. That left one more.

She ripped it open, pulled out a typewritten letter and

froze. It was one sentence: *I know what you did.* She slowly turned it over, looking for any sign of who it came from, then she did the same with the envelope. But there was nothing.

She slowly folded it up, tucked it into the envelope and put it into another folder. She'd labeled that one *Crank*, but it could be so much worse. This was about the seventh one she'd received in seven weeks. She glanced at the calendar and saw it was Wednesday. These letters always came on a Wednesday. She crossed her arms over her chest as she sat here thinking about it. She wondered if she should mention the notes to the cops.

Since the letters always said the same thing, and nothing else happened, she had held off from doing so. But the last thing she wanted was to wait until things got ugly and then to realize she should have done something earlier.

"Is it another one?" Jim held the empty plate in his hand, his face a study of worry as he looked at her. He nodded his head toward the folder in the big file drawer.

"Seven in seven weeks. And of course today's Wednesday. I always get the letter on Wednesday."

With his gaze intent on her face, he said, "Still no idea why you're getting them?"

She shook her head. "No, no clue. And, no, I have no idea what it is I might have done. To say *I know what you did* means nothing to me." She groaned. "I don't need this shit."

"None of us do," he said cheerfully. As he walked out to the main office, he tossed back, "You should probably call the cops. Just saying …"

He was right, but she was still hesitant about that. She didn't have anything to hide, but her life was still … private. And most often, most likely, they would only tell her that they couldn't do anything. And to let them know if anything else developed. The police were most effective *after* a crime was committed, not stopping one from occurring.

She knew guys, like Badger, would have a hissy fit if she tried to ignore this stuff. Most likely Badger and the guys from his unit would have told her to get the harassing notes to the police station, beginning with the first one. Maybe they were right.

She returned her attention to work, trying to ignore the letters, but her mind kept returning to the problem.

She had no idea what the letters referred to. Neither was a date mentioned, was it?

Frowning, she slowly pulled out the last letter and read it again: *I know what you did.* There was no time frame listed. So not what she'd done last summer, last month or last week.

Well, let's see. … She got through school. She'd had sex with a couple strangers in her life, not exactly a high point, but, hey, she hadn't cheated on anyone. She hadn't stolen. She hadn't run anybody over. She stared at the letter, shook her head and tossed it back on top of the others. Whatever it was, it would have to wait. She had more patients coming in.

By the time she had seen two more patients back to back, then had another chance to breathe, she looked up to see three big men walking in. She raised an eyebrow. "I know I get to see you guys a lot, but do any of you have an appointment today?"

She tried to keep her tone light. It was a problem. She was definitely too soft when it came to fitting people in. But in this case, these guys—Badger, Erick and Cade—were all staring at her with goofy grins. She leaned back, crossed her arms over her chest and said, "I'll take that as a no."

"Your office hours are technically over," Badger said.

She looked at him in surprise. "What?" She twisted to look at her computer, and sure enough it was five o'clock. She shook her head. "This has got to stop."

"Yeah, it does," Erick said.

She turned to look at the three of them. "What is it you want?"

"Erick's new leg," Badger said.

She walked to the cabinet and pulled out Erick's prosthetic. He'd been happy with plain-Jane models the whole time, but then he'd wanted the blade runner thing. After watching an old video of somebody in South Africa running in the Olympics on one, and being a bit of a runner himself, he'd wanted to try it. Badger's wasn't quite done, and Erick was waiting on two he'd ordered. She brought one out, took it out of the packaging.

She deliberately had this one toned in a light blue steel. She turned around and handed it over.

He sat down and unbuckled his old prosthetic, his hands eagerly reaching for the new one.

"You guys are just as bad as girls. They like diamonds. You like metal."

The men just nodded. Erick jumped back up onto his legs and took a couple exploratory jumps. A grin filled his face. "Wow, that's supreme."

"You can't have the second one just yet," she said. "I warned you that the top needed to have a different adjustment."

He nodded. "That's all right. I can wait on the second one."

In truth, Erick was missing a foot and the lower leg. Getting his prosthetics had been a godsend in getting his life back. He was also missing two fingers and had a severely damaged shoulder joint. But he always had a big smile on his face.

He walked around the room, hopping on his new leg. She smiled when she realized he wasn't even touching the other foot to the ground. "How does that feel?"

"Awesome." He turned with a big grin and said, "Thanks so much."

She had a small self-conscious moment. The realization that this was why she did what she did. To see these big men find some purpose again, get some joy back in their hearts. "Don't wear this one out so fast," she admonished.

He laughed. "I didn't wear out the last one. It's not my fault there was a weakness in the middle."

She shook her head. "This isn't the standard material for prosthetics anyway. And you well know that. These are heavier. They're also more durable, have better tensile strength, more flexibility ..."

The men turned and headed toward her office door.

She called out, "Cade, I haven't seen you in a long time."

He pivoted to look at her. "I'm having more surgery," he said, his voice grim. "No point in getting fitted until I'm through that process."

She watched the tightness on his face and realized just how hard some of this was for each of these guys. "At least by the time you're done with that stage, we should have a whole new line of prosthetics coming in."

"Yeah? What kind?"

She smiled. "I've designed a couple with pockets, little places you can fit things into, like a cell phone for high up in the thigh. Some weapons." She shrugged. "I don't know where all that will go. I've spent some time talking to Stone about it."

"Now that will be freaking awesome." Cade grinned, his big baby face lighting up. "But it'll still be months."

"And the months would pass anyway," she said gently. "The best thing you can do is heal properly. And, once you're healed," she said, "your adjustment will be very fast. Unlike your blockheaded friend here, who won't get off his leg enough to let his stump heal properly."

The men all grinned, except Badger. He snorted and followed his friends out the door. "Still badgering me, aren't you, Doc? You know you like me."

"I'll badger you all I need to, but I doubt you'll listen," she said with a heavy sigh. She walked out to the main reception area as the men headed toward the front door. She was on the third floor, and she always took the elevator just because she was tired at the end of the day. But she loved to watch the men go down the stairs on her prosthetics. They did it with such grace and style. Maybe it was because of their fitness training; maybe it was their mindset. But they always adjusted very fast. It was gratifying. She leaned against the door, watching them talk among themselves.

Jim came up behind her. "Did you tell them?"

She slid a glance his way. "Tell them what?"

The men stopped at the doorway to the stairs and glanced back. She caught the frown sliding over Badger's face. She turned to head back inside.

"About the threatening letters," Jim protested.

"Of course I didn't," she said as she motioned him inside so the door would shut, and so the men wouldn't hear their conversation. "Why would I? They aren't law enforcement."

He lowered his voice. "Yeah, but I heard they were SEALs."

"*Ark, ark, ark,*" she mocked. "It doesn't matter what they *were*. They're not law enforcement now. And that's all that anybody will care about."

She kept going toward her office, determined to shut down everything for the night. As she turned off the computer, reached for her purse, she turned around to find all three men standing in front of her desk, glaring at her. She glared right back. "What is your problem?"

"You," Badger said. "Yeah, we heard that crack of you imitating a seal."

She grinned. "Got to you, did it?" She gave a quick nod. "Good." She went to move past them. "Maybe you won't be quite so stubborn now when you actually get that bloody leg to heal."

"What's this about threatening letters?" Erick asked.

She shrugged, dismissing his question. She knew they wouldn't be put off, but she'd try. "It's nothing."

Jim snorted.

She turned and glared at him. "If you want to keep your job ..." she threatened in a mocking tone.

"If you get killed, I lose my job anyway," he snapped back. He turned to Erick. "Every Wednesday she's received a threatening letter for seven weeks in a row."

The men straightened and, as one unit, turned to look at her.

She shook her head. "They are hardly threatening letters."

"Let me see them."

She glared at Badger. "Who died and made you boss?"

"You did. The minute you didn't tell us about the damn letters in the first place."

"When was I supposed to tell you?" she protested. There

was only one way to deal with this. The men wouldn't walk away until they saw the letters, so all she had to do was show them and point out it was nothing to be worried about, and they'd leave. Well, she hoped they would. She pulled out the file and grabbed the letters. "They're all the same. They come every Wednesday, and I have no idea what they mean." She handed the stack to Badger.

He read the first one and passed it over to Erick, who read it and passed it to Cade. Badger quickly went through all seven and then turned to look at her. "No idea what they mean or what they refer to?"

She shook her head. "That's one of the reasons why I didn't tell the cops. I don't have a clue what they refer to. Nobody'll believe me because these letters imply I did something wrong or did something I'm ashamed of. I don't have a clue."

The men studied her face intently for a long moment, and then Badger gave a decisive nod. "I believe you."

"Gee, thanks," she said in a droll tone.

He shook a finger at her. "Don't be like that. You never know when you'll need a friend."

She leaned forward, placed her palms flat on her desk and glared at him. "And that goes double for you. You never know when you will need a friend."

Silence fell in her office.

BACK OUTSIDE, ERICK and Cade turned to face Badger. "What the hell was that last comment she made about?"

He shrugged irritably. "Who knows?"

But the men wouldn't be put off. Erick shook his head.

"Oh, no you don't. She made a comment as if you had no friends."

"She thinks my friends aren't enough to keep me alive."

The men stopped at the truck and stared at him.

He raised both hands in frustration. "She thinks I've got a death wish. That any attempt I make toward finding out what asshole did this to us will end with me dying. She's trying to get me to think my friends aren't enough to keep me alive because then I'll turn away from my mission." He knew his buddies would understand. They were his friends after all. Regardless of what she said, he did have good ones.

"I gather she cares?" Erick asked. He hit the button on his remote and heard the locks unlocking on his truck up ahead. "Too bad. I was thinking about asking her out."

"Go ahead," Badger said, unable to keep surliness from his tone. "So far all she's done is nag."

At that, Erick and Cade grinned. "Sounds like you care."

Badger shrugged. But he'd been wondering the same thing. He turned to look up at the office to see her standing there, arms crossed, staring at them. He lifted a hand and waved. But she didn't move. He knew there was something between them; he just didn't know what. And the trouble was, if he took a step in that direction, it would pull him away from his main focus. She wasn't a one-night-stand kind of girl. She was a staying-around kind of girl. And he couldn't even think about staying. He knew what he was doing was dangerous as all hell.

For the longest time he hadn't given a shit, considering his busted-ass body. He'd have been happy to have found the answers to his questions even if it killed him. He knew it would bother her, but she'd get over it. What he couldn't afford to lose was his focus. To lose that sense of direction.

Yet it *was* a good way to get a man killed. And, yeah, he
knew that meant he was considering keeping himself alive
through all this. He wasn't doing this as a suicide mission.
But, if that's what happened, up until now he'd been good
with it.

Cade smacked Badger on the shoulder. "What are you
thinking about?"

He gave his head a shake and stood glaring at them, only
to realize he was a good six feet from the truck, and Erick
already had the door open. Badger groaned. "That woman's
making me crazy."

"That's a good sign."

"Like hell it is." He hopped into the back seat of the
truck. It was a big F350 with a full bench seat in the back. It
was about the only size vehicle that fit the three of them.
They'd always been some of the bigger men in the unit.
They weren't all oversized, like Badger was, but still it took a
lot of vehicle space to stop them from sitting in each other's
laps.

"Yes, it's a good sign. She cares that you care. But what's
holding you two apart?" Cade asked.

"Hey, maybe they should be apart." Erick gave a laugh.
"That gives me a chance."

Cade shook his head. "She didn't even look at you. Well,
she did, but she was more concerned with your busted-ass
body than she was with who you were."

"I'm good if she's looking at my body." Erick gave another big laugh.

Badger settled back. He let his friends do their talking,
always with the lighthearted banter. It helped them get
through the darker moments. "She might even go out with
you," he said to Erick.

Cade shook his head. "Hell, no, she won't. It'll be you or nobody."

Badger glanced over at him. "You're nuts."

"Nope. You're just being blind."

"Doesn't matter. It would be foolish to get involved at this stage."

"What will you do?"

"Road trip," he said succinctly. "And I'm not taking her with me."

"Maybe you should. Sounds like she's got more trouble than she can handle here. Without anybody to watch her back, she might as well go with you just to get away and stay safe."

He resettled in his seat and stared out the big windows. "No, that would be *putting* her in danger. I won't do that."

"Maybe you should give her that choice."

He shook his head. "Hell no. Besides, she's got a business here and lots of guys like us who need her."

There wasn't much the others could say to that because Badger was right. She had a busy practice. To just pick up and pull out wouldn't be easy.

"Anybody got any idea what those letters mean?"

"She says she doesn't have a clue. But she must. I understand wanting to keep her privacy, but, if this goes from bad to worse, privacy won't keep her safe."

"I can't imagine she did anything. She's one of those super-squeaky-clean scared-to-do-anything-wrong always-walk-on-the-right-side-of-life type people."

"Clean, innocent and naive," Badger said. "And we need people like her. To give a freshness to the air around us. People like that are the reason we did what we did."

"And what we're still doing," Cade said.

Erick turned the engine on. "That's the thing, isn't it? We're all out of work. We've spent the last couple years getting our bodies back together, and we really haven't done anything else. What the hell are we going to do now?"

"We can always work with Levi," Cade said with a note of humor. But there was also enough seriousness in his tone that the others knew it was a viable proposition.

"The trouble is, he's already got plenty of guys, and they're probably in a lot better shape than we are."

"Just because I've got a prosthetic arm and leg," Cade said, "doesn't mean I'm any less a man than the others."

Badger grinned. "Hell, you're way more than the others. By the time she's done tinkering with all our prosthetics, we'll be bionic men."

Cade gave him a nod of satisfaction. "See? That's why we've got to keep her safe. Otherwise we have to get a new doc to fix our stuff."

"But keeping her safe—what does that mean?" Erick asked as he drove the big truck out into the main traffic and turned right at the next intersection. "Is she in danger? I don't like those letters any more than the next guy, but every Wednesday? There's obviously some significance to that."

"Significance, yes, but we don't know why. Maybe he only gets one window to write and mail letters? We can only guess."

"In that case it would be a Monday or Tuesday, depending on where he lived."

Just as he pulled into the back of the parking lot of a local pub, Badger's phone went off. He pulled it out, looked at the number and said, "It's Kat."

Erick turned off the engine. Instead of getting out, he twisted in his seat, propping his arm on the seat back and asked, "What's up?"

Badger shrugged and hit Talk. "Kat, what's up?" But there was no answer. "Kat? ... Hello?" He slowly raised his gaze to the other two men. "Her number came up. But there was no answer."

"Did you hear any breathing? Did you hear a sound on the other end?"

Badger shook his head. "It's almost as if the person hung up right away. But there was no dial tone to tell me it was dead."

Erick turned around in his seat and turned the engine back on. "I suggest we go check."

In the meantime, Badger hit Redial. It rang and rang. "Now she's not answering." He quickly called the second office number, hoping somebody, like Jim, would answer. But it rang and rang too. "The office is closed for the day now, isn't it?"

"Yeah, we should have brought her with us," Cade growled. "Especially after reading those letters."

"The letters didn't say anything. And there was no indication anything was about to happen. Yes, it's Wednesday, and she got her seventh letter. But again we don't know what that means." Erick's voice was terse, but his words were sensible.

When he couldn't get the feeling inside to go away, Badger knew something was majorly wrong. He'd received lots of pocket phone calls; this didn't feel the same. It felt worse.

They were only minutes away. By the time Erick parked on the side street around the corner from the office building, Badger was already out, racing toward the front of the building. Erick and Cade joined him.

"Is there another entrance into the building?" Erick asked. "Of course there is, but do we know where?"

Badger nodded and veered off to the side. "It's this way."

The back door was locked. But, as it was, the janitor was unloading mop buckets and a box of cleansers. They waited until he opened the rear door and called out, "Thank you," and bolted toward Kat's office. When they arrived, her door was locked. All the lights behind the glass were turned off. Erick brushed them aside. "Let me get this."

"There should be a security system," Cade warned.

Erick nodded. "Of course there is." He had the door open in seconds.

Badger had no idea how long they had before the alarm went off. They raced to the back of the office where the alarm panel was mounted on the wall. A count of seventeen seconds remained. Nobody was in the office that they could see. But while Erick worked on the security system, Badger and Cade did the full sweep. "It's empty," Cade called out.

"And the security system was never reset. So it wouldn't have gone off," Erick snapped, appearing in front of them, his face grim. "The only reason she wouldn't have set it for the night is if she couldn't. She's got hundreds of thousands of dollars' worth of equipment here."

"But it's all very specialized. It's not like something somebody could come in, scoop up and sell on the black market."

Badger studied her lab setup. "Nothing appears to be disturbed. Nobody's here. Outside of the fact the door was locked, and the security was not set, that could be just because we rattled her about those letters earlier. Maybe nothing's wrong."

But he knew that wasn't true. He swept an arm toward

the empty building. "Let's make sure her vehicle isn't parked in her spot, then head to her place to see if she made it home."

The three men chose to go down the front stairs, out the front door. But there was no sign anything had happened to Kat, and her vehicle was no longer parked in her spot. Back in the truck, the trip to her place took almost as long as it took to get to the pub. In other words, it took nothing. She only lived about six blocks away. He'd found that out months ago. They pulled up outside the small two-story house that had the appearance of a bygone era with a large veranda at the front of the house with gardens off to the side. It was a large block, and the neighbors were set back a ways.

The three men got out of the vehicle and walked past the house, being careful to not look at it. The last thing they wanted was to give any kidnappers an inkling they'd been seen if there was a hostage situation inside. When they spied the alleyway, that played into their hands beautifully.

They walked around the block to the east, coming up the alley until they reached the neighbors beside Kat's house. From there they peered over the fence, studying the layout of Kat's property. A garage was in the front, and the door had been closed, so, if Kat's vehicle was in there or not, nobody knew. A side door led into the garage. Somebody needed to get in there and check for her car. If she hadn't made it home, they needed to track that vehicle, and they needed to track it now.

Badger said in a low voice, "I'll check out the garage. Be back in two." He hopped over the fence, barely holding back his cry of pain as he came down hard on his sore leg. He'd heal. Eventually. Or maybe Kat was right. He should give it a little time before he went for another run. On the other hand, if running would save her life, he was up to being a marathon runner today.

He slipped across to the garage and reached for the door knob—locked. He quickly pulled out the kit he carried in his back pocket, and had it open in seconds. He froze. A vehicle was in her garage. But it sure as hell wasn't hers.

CHAPTER 4

ERRIFIED, KAT SAT on her own kitchen chair as the man behind her held a gun to her head and a finger to his lips. A cloth rag was tied around her mouth to keep her from screaming. She didn't know what they might have seen or heard, but, all of a sudden, instead of leaving her as she was, they tied her up. As soon as she was secured, the two men split in opposite directions, both with weapons out, checking the lower floor of her house. They'd already checked it once, but obviously they were looking for something different now. She didn't know who they were. They'd accosted her as she was getting into her vehicle at work.

She'd been picked up, tossed in the trunk of their car and taken home. That they even knew where her home was, was terrifying. She'd tried to contact somebody for help on her phone by hitting Redial. Whoever the hell that was. But she'd lost her phone when the vehicle had careened around the corner.

She leaned her head back, thinking. She didn't know who the men were, but they obviously knew who she was. The obvious conclusion was this had something to do with the letters. But it could just as easily have something to do with the three men who came to her office earlier. She was well aware Badger was on a dangerous mission. Were these men after Badger? Or were these the men Badger was after?

Not that it made any difference to her right now. She had to get through this. The last thing she wanted was to die in her own home as a captive.

She didn't know if these men knew she was missing a leg herself. She hoped not. While she'd been designing others' prosthetics, she'd been working hard to improve her own. She still had a few tricks to play, but she had to get her legs free first.

The larger of the two gunmen who'd been looking out the front windows came past her and headed toward the kitchen. She could hear them whispering that they heard sounds in the backyard and thought they saw somebody peering over the fence. That could be anything from nosy Dorothy down at the end of the alley to Badger, who had, for whatever fictional tale she wanted to conjure up in her head, come looking for her.

Her mouth was so dry. She was desperate for some water. She was also exhausted after her long day. She didn't realize how much those letters were having a negative effect on her system. Just dealing with the issue was depressing.

The two men came through the kitchen, headed for the stairs, then ran to the second floor. She watched them, frowning. The second man was much slimmer, smaller. She'd call him more of a monkey of a man. He reminded her of one of the old-style chimneysweeps. Something was creepy and dirty about him. The larger of the two men was better dressed, had better diction, appeared to have a little more money and a little more self-care. But something about his exaggeratedly large teeth sent shivers down her back.

They hadn't touched her other than to pick her up and tie her down. But she knew, with night falling, their minds would turn to something else. And that was when she would get her chance. In order to rape her, they'd have to untie her from the chair. She just needed a few moments with her leg free; then she could possibly save herself. She didn't think anybody was coming to rescue her.

Just as she figured that, she glanced around, hearing something behind her. Twisting she caught sight of a face in the glass panel of the door that led to the garage. She froze.

She didn't know if she should be happy or terrified. She didn't think her two kidnappers were expecting a visitor. The last thing she wanted was to consider a third asshole was party to her kidnapping. But she couldn't imagine who else it could be at her door.

When she heard a *snick*, she realized the door was opening. She knew the men had locked it behind them because the bigger guy had ordered the little one to do it. She presumed he had followed that order; otherwise, how did they pull off these kinds of criminal acts?

Her neck was really hurting. She couldn't keep looking around the corner. But when she heard footsteps ever-so-slight behind her, she twisted again. Her gaze was wide and terrified, and her gagged mouth opened a bit in shock, but no sound came out.

Badger stood beside her. He put a finger to his lips and whispered, "How many?"

With her hands tied behind her back, she lifted two fingers and squeezed the rest into a fist. He noted her actions and held up two fingers. She nodded. He pointed up the stairs, and she nodded. He held his finger back to his lips and disappeared out the door, the way he'd come in.

Her heart pounded; hope raced through her bloodstream, but she didn't understand why he was leaving. And without her.

But she sure as hell hoped it was to get some help. No sooner had that thought entered her mind when two men came through the door. Had they been seen?

Erick stood in front of her. Pulling out his pocketknife, he quickly cut the ties around her ankles and wrists. At the same time, Cade loosened the gag on her mouth. Cade helped her to her feet and tugged her toward the door. She twisted to look at the other two men, not wanting to leave without them. Badger waved her off. And she realized his focus was already on the men upstairs. Just then she heard running footsteps. Cade pulled her out of the house and into the garage. He took the knife and plunged it into the tire closest to him and walked around to do the same to the others. With the vehicle disabled, he tugged her to the back of the garage and out the door. He helped her over the fence and then hopped the fence into the neighbor's yard with her. Within seconds he gently pushed her into the back seat of a truck.

She slid inside, her voice and breath raspy and harsh. "How did you guys know?"

"Didn't you call Badger?"

She stared at him in surprise. "I hit Redial. But I never got a chance to say anything. They turned a really hard corner, and I got slammed up against the inside of their trunk and lost the phone in the darkness."

"Did you hear it ringing again?"

"I don't think so. They were probably already dragging me into my house by then."

"We need to get your phone back. Is it in the trunk?"

"Yes. You should help Badger and Erick."

Cade laughed. "They'd consider that an insult, by the

way."

She stared at him. "What? Why would that be insulting?"

"The two of them against two kidnappers. That's easy odds for our guys."

She shook her head. "The kidnappers are armed. I forgot to tell him that. They have guns."

"That's all right. Our guys do too."

Her jaw dropped open as he pulled a pistol from a shoulder holster under his jacket. "Are you allowed to carry that?"

"Yep, we are. It's one of the reasons we were contemplating going to Texas. Working for Levi. It would help us continue to do the same work we've always done, and we get to carry guns." He plastered a grin on his face.

Was it to make light of a job that allowed him to carry guns? She shook her head and leaned back. "You guys are crazy."

"You are the one who got kidnapped."

She reached a hand to her temple. "I certainly didn't mean to. They grabbed me when I was getting in my car."

"So obviously you were targeted. They caught you just after you left the office and before you made it home. They could have caught you in your office, or they could have also caught you at your house. So why the vehicle?"

He spoke in such a contemplative voice that she realized he was seriously trying to figure out the kidnappers' thought process.

"I was just about to start my car when," she admitted. "I realized I forgot to set the alarm."

"Yes, you did. We've already been through your office."

She stared at him in shock. "How did you get inside?"

He gave her a droll look. "Have you forgotten what we used to do?"

She shook her head slowly. "No, I just hadn't considered the applications in today's world or how it might impact me."

"Well, now you have firsthand experience," he said cheerfully.

But she knew the whole time he was talking to her in that light pleasing tone, his gaze was searching all around the area. "Are you expecting them back right away?"

"Of course I am," he said. "But I'm not expecting any trouble taking out the kidnappers."

"Of course there will be trouble," she said wearily. "We'll be lucky if there isn't one or two of them sporting bullet holes."

"I don't give a damn about the two kidnappers. But my boys, they had better not be sporting any."

Just then Cade's phone went off. He pulled it out, gave a nod of satisfaction and said, "It's Badger." He hit the Speaker button and said, "Badger, what's up?"

"You can bring her back in. We have two kidnappers trussed up in the kitchen. Would be nice if we had some information from her so we know how to proceed."

She was already out the door and standing on the sidewalk, waiting for Cade. Together the two walked around the corner and in the front door. As they walked to the kitchen, Kat realized that the two men were now sitting on kitchen chairs tied up like sheep. She grinned at them. "Fancy meeting you here like this."

The two men just glared her.

"Do you know these two men?" Badger asked.

She shook her head and quickly brought him up on the

details of how she'd been kidnapped.

He nodded and tossed her a wallet. "The big one's name is Paul Keiling."

"If you can believe that. Isn't it easy for them to get fake IDs these days?" She studied the driver's license in the front window of the wallet. It was well done and looked passably close to him. "Maybe it is him?" She went through the rest of his wallet, hoping he had a couple credit cards, but inside, tucked in the back, was one of those secret flaps. And in there she pulled out a note.

Paul struggled against his bonds when he saw her do that.

She waved it in front of him. "Oh, is this something you don't want me to see?" She handed the wallet to Erick for him to peruse. She quickly opened up the note and let out a silent whistle. To the rest of the men she read, "I know what you did." And she held it up for the others to see. She glanced down at the big man. "So, are you the one who's been sending me those notes?"

From the blank look in his eyes, she realized he didn't know anything about them. But something else was going on in the back of his gaze. What would make a man kidnap her like he had? On a hunch, she pulled up a chair and sat in front of him. "Have you been getting these?"

He nodded slowly.

"So have I. Are you getting one a week?"

The big man nodded again slowly.

She nodded. "Yeah, me too. Mine comes every Wednesday. What about yours?"

He nodded.

She sat back, her fingers dancing up and down on her arm as she contemplated him. "So, I guess the question here is, what did you do?"

This time he just glared at her, that same bullish look coming back into his eyes as she'd seen before, and his lips pinched shut.

BADGER WANTED TO laugh at the sour look on the kidnapper's face. But that same sense of laughter was a very thin cover over the anger that fired through his system. What kind of an asshole would kidnap a woman, especially one like Kat? She did such good with her work; everybody needed her skills. And these assholes were hell-bent on taking her out of the picture. He leaned forward and gripped Paul's throat in his big fist. "What were you going to do with her?"

Paul gasped and choked, but Badger didn't relent. He knew the asshole would have shot Kat. Badger had to get to the bottom of this, and he had to get there now.

The other man spoke up. "We were following orders."

Badger stepped back slightly and looked at him. "Whose orders?"

Both men shrugged. Paul said, "I got a letter. I was told to kidnap her and keep her prisoner in this house. Otherwise he'd tell."

"And what was he going to do with her?"

Silence.

Kat got up and walked nervously around the kitchen. She had her arms wrapped around her chest as if to keep warm.

But Badger knew the chill wasn't on the outside. It was on the inside. He gently stroked her back. "Remember that it's okay. We found you in time."

She gave a small nod and a grateful smile. "But how do *I* handle the nightmares when I wake up realizing how close I came to not being found?"

He understood because he woke up with nightmares consuming him over the bomb that blew apart his truck. There really was no good answer for her. "Time. It will ease back with time."

She gave him a small smile and looked back at the two kidnappers. "How did he give you your instructions?"

The smaller man answered. "He's had seven letters. Today he got an eighth one. But this one told him that he needed to snatch you off the street and bring you back to the house and keep you here until we receive further instructions."

Badger immediately checked the time on his watch.

"We?" Erick asked, pouncing on his turn of phrase.

The smaller man shrugged. "Paul's a buddy of mine. I wouldn't leave him to deal with this on his own."

Badger studied the two of them. Even in the darker side of life, everyone needed to have friends. Maybe Kat was right. Maybe he should consider friendship over vengeance. But it was damn hard.

Cade studied the two kidnappers. "Were there any other instructions?"

The smaller man shook his head. "Not yet. We only just got here."

Badger studied his face for a long moment, wondering if he was telling the truth. Finally he decided there was no deceit in the man's voice or eyes. Then again they'd been caught. No point in lying at this stage. He glanced at his buddies and caught their slight nods. He looked back to Kat to see her frowning at him.

"What are you up to?" she asked in a harsh tone.

He just grinned at her. How she knew so much about him and could understand who he was on the inside, he didn't know. Maybe it was because she was the doc. Maybe it was because she dealt with guys like him all the time. On the other hand, he'd like to think there weren't a ton of guys just like him. But, for whatever reason, she got under his skin and seemed to understand who he was. He motioned at the two men tied up on chairs. "The man pulling their strings hasn't checked in yet to see if they were successful."

She tapped her foot on the floor and gazed at him. "And ..."

"And ..." he said, crossing his arms over his chest as he studied her, "if we all stay where we are, there's a good chance he will contact them with further instructions of what they're supposed to do with you."

Her gaze widened into understanding. "And you're thinking we can capture him then?"

He shrugged. "I don't know about the timing, but capturing him would obviously be the end result we would like to achieve. He might just give them more instructions."

She turned to look at her two kidnappers. "Do we trust them?" Both men tried to put trustworthy looks on their faces. She snorted. "Of course we can't trust you."

"Hey," Paul said, "I wouldn't have laid a hand on you if I hadn't had my back pushed to the wall."

She glared at him. "But you did lay a hand on me. And I won't forget that kind of terror easily."

Cade stepped forward and held out her phone. "In all this mess, I forgot I retrieved this for you."

Her face lit up as she reached for her phone. "Awesome." She swiped the top glass, and her smile fell away.

In two seconds Badger was at her side. "What's wrong?"

She shrugged irritably. "I didn't say anything was wrong. I missed a text."

"I didn't text you, but I called your phone, and of course you didn't answer." He watched her face as she went through her phone.

She clicked on something, and her lips thinned. "This is the first text communication I've had from him." She held up her phone so Badger could see. It was the same messages as on the letters. **I know what you did.**

He read that statement out loud. Then turned to look at the two kidnappers.

Both focused on Kat with an interested look on their faces.

Paul said, "I am not talking about that, but I'd sure be interested in knowing what you did."

She raised both hands. "I wish I knew what he was talking about too. I didn't do anything. I'm not a thief. I didn't sleep with anybody's husband …"

Paul snorted. "Well, I don't know that I believe you. He obviously thinks he has something worth doing this for."

She tapped her foot on the floor. "How long ago did whatever you did happen?"

Her question was a little convoluted, but Badger understood she was figuring out a time frame here.

Paul said, "Last summer."

She frowned. "Do we know anybody else affected by this guy?"

Paul shook his head. "No. Why?"

"I'm looking for a time frame that I could search my diary and see if something went down that maybe he's thinking I did. I honestly haven't a clue what he's talking about." She turned around and said, "Where did my purse and keys go?"

The two kidnappers shrugged. "Probably still in your car where we picked you up."

She frowned. "That's possible." Suddenly she looked nervous. She turned to Badger. "I need to get those as soon as possible."

Cade stepped forward. "Your car wasn't in its usual spot at the office. Where is it now?"

"I was about to turn the car on when these two idiots grabbed me." She glared at the smaller man, the one prone to take orders.

"I drove your car here, following Paul, but it's parked down the block."

Cade nodded. "I'll be a few minutes." He slipped out the back way.

Badger loved working with these two. They didn't have to be told how or why or what to do. He wished he had some idea what was going on here. He knew the general logistics, but, if she couldn't come up with something she'd done, then it made him wonder just how severe an incident this guy was talking about. He checked his watch for the time once more. "Do you guys have any idea what the blackmailer's ultimately looking for?"

Paul shook his head. "No. I was pretty pissed when I started getting the letters," he admitted. "But, the bottom line is, I just wanted him to go away. When I was told to collect her, I was hoping that would be the end of it."

"But you know it's not going to be. Chances are good he might have wanted her killed."

He ignored the soft gasp of dismay from Kat. She was holding on, waffling between anger and tears. He wanted the anger to win. He was no good when it came to women in tears. The other men seemed to look at her sideways, like she was a bomb about to go off. He figured they couldn't handle crying women either.

Paul shook his head. "I don't think there's any point in that. The only reason to do something like this is if he could get something from us. Obviously he needed somebody to kidnap her. But what can he get from her?"

Everyone turned to look at Kat. She shrugged. "It depends."

But her tone had changed. Badger stepped forward, reached out a hand and tilted her chin so she looked at him. "It depends on what?"

She sighed. "It depends if he knows about the rare coins I inherited."

CHAPTER 5

S HE HADN'T WANTED anyone to know about them. The fact that they were gold coins from the 1800s meant they were worth a ton of money. She had six of them.

She cast a glance around the room, everyone staring at her. "They were an inheritance from my great uncle," she announced. "No, I didn't kill him. No, I didn't steal them. I have no idea if that's what this guy is talking about or not. But I don't know anything negative connected with them. I didn't know they existed until my great uncle died."

"How did your uncle die?"

She winced. "He was murdered."

Dead silence followed.

"An intruder broke into the house and shot him. The police suspected it was a botched burglary attempt." She reached up a hand to brush tendrils of hair from her temple. "And, if you guys think I killed him, you couldn't be more wrong."

"Did the suspicion ever fall on you?"

She shrugged. "I think the suspicion fell on everyone at one point. They never found out who did it, so that's still something. He lived in town, so I had the opportunity. He was murdered early evening, and I was at home alone. So, as far as the police were concerned, I had a motive in the sense that I inherited his coins. But I didn't know I was inheriting the coins, and that's because I didn't know he even had the coins."

"We need to get a hold of that police file."

She gave a harsh laugh. "Good luck with that. I can't even get them to give me an update on my uncle's case."

"Who gave you the coins?"

She shrugged. "My uncle's lawyer."

"And what about the rest of your uncle's estate? Who got that?"

"His second wife. His much-younger wife. She was pissed when she found out I got the coins."

"No love lost between you?"

Kat shook her head and stared down at the floor. How did she explain the strange relationship between her uncle and his new wife? "My uncle was married for thirty years, happily married. But Aunt Ethel died from breast cancer four maybe five years ago now. Before I knew it, he was suddenly married to this woman, Marge."

"You don't like her?"

She lifted her gaze to study Badger. "I don't know. I haven't really given her a chance. I loved Aunt Ethel. It was a blow to lose her. Particularly the way she died. And then when my uncle suddenly turned around and seemed to have dealt with it all so quickly, it made me suspicious that maybe he'd been carrying on with Marge before Aunt Ethel's death. For the longest time I didn't talk to him, in case I accused him of just that. But he seemed so damn happy, it was hard to be upset with him. He'd gone through hell with Aunt Ethel during those last eighteen months of her life. If he could find a little bit of happiness, then who was I to question him?"

She hoped Badger believed her. But, at the same time,

she knew the police had had trouble with it. "I will say," she added quietly, "Marge did try to throw some of the blame on my shoulders."

Badger's eyebrows went straight up. "Why?"

"Because she was pissed about the coins, I think," Kat said. "But I can't be too sure."

He nodded absentmindedly. "It's possible this person believes you killed your uncle in order to get the coins."

"Does everyone just turn around and kill their family in the hopes they get something? I had no reason to think he would be leaving me anything. He has no kids, and, in fact, he probably made Marge a very wealthy woman."

"That bothers you?"

"It shouldn't. But there's that little bit of doubt that she had something to do with my uncle's murder, so, if she did, I would hope to God she wouldn't get to keep the spoils of her actions."

"You know the detective handling your case?"

"If I can get my purse back, I have his card."

Just then the door opened, and Cade stepped inside. He held up her purse. "It looks like it was untouched." He handed her the purse and car keys.

"Thank you so much," she cried out happily. She pocketed the keys and went through her purse. "Credit card and cash are all in here," she said with relief. "I was so afraid I'd have to redo all my cards again."

"Again?"

She turned to Badger. "Yes, I had my purse stolen a few months ago."

The three men exchanged glances.

She looked at them and frowned. "Why?"

"Well, it gives whoever stole them your full name, your

address"—Badger waved his arm around the property—"potentially access to the property. You'd be surprised what guys can find out about a woman through her purse."

She stared at him, her jaw dropping slowly. "I just don't think the way you guys do."

"Neither do you think like a criminal, and that's a good thing. But it also makes you naive." He motioned at the purse in her hand. "Do you have the detective's card?"

She sat down with her purse on her lap, going through the pockets. "Here it is." She pulled it out and handed it to Erick.

Erick looked down at it. "Laramie Birch." He frowned and handed it to Badger. "I've never heard of him."

"We don't know many cops here," Badger said. He stared at the card. "Might be time we developed a network in town."

"In Santa Fe, New Mexico?" Kat shrugged. "The only point to developing a network here is if you're planning on staying. And, as we all know, you're heading off on a fool's errand, getting yourself killed."

He snapped the card in his hand, making a sharp sound. "You don't know anything."

"I know you can lose everything you have on that fool's errand."

"I have to do this," he insisted.

She stared at him for a long moment, and then her shoulders sagged in defeat. "Fine, do it. But it would be awfully damn nice if you came home alive and healthy."

His tone mocking, he said, "And here I thought you'd be happy to see me leave." He slyly checked his watch.

She glared at him. "I will be, provided I don't get into any more trouble with assholes like these two." She turned to glare at the two kidnappers. "What did you two do that this guy is concerned about?"

Paul shook his head. His face was bland, too bland.

She stared at him suspiciously. "I don't suppose you're the one who shot my uncle, are you?"

He stared at her in horror, but a flash of panic crossed his face.

She groaned. "Please, no. ... Please tell me that you didn't actually kill my uncle."

He shook his head. "I don't know anything about your uncle."

She snorted. "So, if it wasn't my uncle, you shot somebody else, didn't you?"

In a fatalistic move his shoulders sagged, and he stared at her. After a long moment he slowly nodded his head. "Yes. I did."

BADGER WATCHED THE color slide away from Kat's cheeks. It was one thing to contemplate a murderer, particularly when she'd been on the receiving end of a family member being murdered, but it was another thing to stare them in the face. She looked shocked. And cold.

She wrapped her arms around her chest again and walked away from the man several paces. Then she suddenly turned and looked back at him. "Did you plan to kill this person?"

Paul shook his head. "No, I didn't. We went in there looking for something easy to lift. Something we could pawn for a few dollars. My friend needed a fix. He'd been trying to get off the drugs, and we were weaning him slowly. Smaller doses each time. But it was expensive even then. We went in looking for TVs, cameras, cell phones, anything we could just grab and run. But the owner had a gun. He shot my partner, and I shot him."

Badger watched the man's face and read the truth in his statement. "Unfortunately it happens all too often, doesn't it?"

Paul nodded. "I wish I'd been anywhere else that day. But I can't undo what I did."

"Do you know for sure that you killed him?" Kat asked.

Badger wanted to smile, but it was too serious a moment. Even now Kat was searching for some light in this dark situation.

Paul shrugged. "I didn't stick around to find out. I picked up my buddy and left. I dropped him off at the hospital, but he was dead within hours. And he never gave a statement. I did call the police and let them know that there'd been a break-in and that I'd heard shooting. But I didn't do a follow-up. I was too scared. I could get life."

"Who else would know you were there that day?" Badger asked. "Because whoever is sending the letters knows this, I assume."

"I don't know that he does." Kat's voice was thoughtful. "He could just be fishing. Why did he choose Paul? Maybe he saw him running from the house. Maybe he saw him at the hospital. Hell, he could have been one of the doctors in the emergency room. There are all kinds of scenarios. But everyone feels guilty over something. The letter writer didn't give a time frame, and he didn't mention a specific incident. He left it broad and general. It spikes fear in all of us."

Paul glared at her. "Even you?"

She stared at him. "I certainly haven't been a saint. But

outside of being mean to kids in school when I was younger, hitting back at a boyfriend who'd hurt me badly, things like that, I can't think of a single incident that was criminal or even ghosted along the edge of being criminal."

There was so much honesty on her face and in her voice that Badger believed her.

"But there was one incident …" She lifted a hand to her temple and massaged it gently.

Everyone froze and stared at her.

"I was at a conference a year ago. I have patents for my designs. But I was accused at the conference of stealing somebody else's design. My patent had been submitted earlier than his, which was about the only thing I had as proof that I hadn't stolen anything. But it did leave a sour taste in my mouth."

"Could it be that simple?"

She shrugged. "I have no idea. It was one of the ugliest things I've ever had to go through. And I have no idea why he would have assumed I had stolen his work. But of course he proclaimed it publicly and loudly. I was one of the speakers, and I think it was done to discredit me." She made a face. "I'm sure you can imagine how unpleasant that whole four-day conference was after that."

Erick glared at the group of them. "None of this makes any sense. And I really hate it when things aren't logical."

Badger nodded. "I agree. We need to get to the bottom of this." He checked his watch yet again.

"What are you checking the time for?" Kat asked.

"The kidnappers are here. They have you here. They're waiting for their next set of instructions. We don't know what the end game is, but, if we can keep the game in play, we have a better chance of catching whoever's doing this."

Paul nodded. "He's right. And I'm game. I'd like to get this asshole out of my life too."

"The trouble is, you're also hoping to get away with murder," Kat said in a caustic tone of voice. "I'm pretty sure that guy's family is looking for closure to what you did."

Paul's shoulders stiffened. "I get that," he said quietly. "I certainly didn't plan on having to shoot somebody that day."

"So why did you take a gun then?" Erick asked, his tone casual as he stared at the guy.

"I didn't. My friend did. I didn't even know he was carrying at the time. Like I said, we were just looking for something we could get quick cash for. And, before you say it, yes, I know we could get jobs and pay for the drugs that way. The thing is, I had a job, only I wasn't earning enough for his drug habit too. But I was trying to help a friend, and, as my buddy here has just found out, helping a friend is often not in his own best interests." Paul pointed to his skinny accomplice. "You should let him go. He's got nothing to do with this."

The small guy said, "Hey, don't say that. I'm just as involved as you are."

"And you shouldn't be," Paul said. "Now you'll have a kidnapping charge on your head. Prison is not for the faint of heart."

"And you know that from personal experience, do you?" Cade asked, his voice almost startling because he'd been quiet for the last half an hour.

Paul turned to look at him and shook his head. "No, I don't have a record. No, I've never done jail time. But my brother did. When he came out, he was a different man."

Badger had heard the same thing time and again. It wasn't an easy life. Being incarcerated with other criminals, some of them a hell of a lot worse who didn't give a shit whether they lived or died, made day-to-day jailhouse living perilous.

Just then a phone rang. Everybody reached in their pockets. When Badger realized the phone belonged to one of the kidnappers, he nodded at Paul. "Do you need to answer that?"

The guy gave him a hard look. "I have no idea who it is, so how am I supposed to know?"

Cade fished the phone out of Paul's pocket and held it up. "It's an unidentified caller." He hit Talk and held it to Paul's ear.

Paul said, "Hello?"

"Have you got her?"

The way Cade was holding the phone it was easy for everyone in the room to hear.

Paul said, "Yeah, I do."

"Good. Now kill her."

There was one sound and one sound only in that room. And that was Kat's cry, "No. Please, no."

Badger knew it was less in response to the actual thought of being killed than to the thought that somebody could hate her so much, and possibly it was a voice she might have recognized. He gave her hand a shake, willing her to look at him so he didn't have to speak. When she turned her huge eyes toward him, he mouthed, *Do you know that speaker?* Slowly she nodded her head, and his eyebrows rose. He bent down so her mouth was against his ear.

She whispered, "It's my brother."

CHAPTER 6

B ADGER'S ARM CAME around her shoulders, pulling her
close to him. Without his support she was sure she'd
have crumpled to the ground. Her mind kept reeling,
searching for an answer. But her heart already knew.

It was her brother. A brother she hadn't seen or heard
from in a long time. But there was no mistaking the way he
spoke. He had a weird slur, something to do with his tooth
alignment. He'd always had it.

But it didn't make any sense that he'd try to kill her. Or
try to have her killed.

Badger just held her close. She wanted to hear the rest of
the conversation. She twisted to look at Paul. "Did he say
anything else?"

Slowly Paul shook his head. "No. He didn't give me a
chance to speak either."

She glanced at Erick and Cade. But their laptops were
open on the kitchen table, and they pounded the keys
furiously. "What are they doing?" she asked Badger.

"They're tracing the call."

"He wasn't on long enough, was he?"

Badger slid her a sideways glance. "What do you know
about tracing calls?"

"Only what I've seen on TV shows. About the caller
having to be on the line long enough for somebody to trace

it." She frowned. "It was an unidentified caller number."

"Sure, but we can get that number. There are ways to get almost anything now." He turned toward Erick. "You did get a number, didn't you?"

Erick nodded. "I did. Which is pretty stupid on his part. So he's either about to toss the phone, or he's really cocky and doesn't have a clue what he's doing. I'll lock in on his location now per his phone."

"If it's who I think it is," Kat said, "then he might know more than we think. My brother has been in and out of jail. I think he went in the last time three years ago."

"Your brother?" the small wiry man asked. "Holy shit, this is getting ugly."

"*If* it's him, it's always been ugly. I come from a split family—two mothers, one father, one child from each mother."

"And I gather the two of you never got along."

"He was older than me. He was smarter than me. He was my father's favorite because he was a male and had the same attitude toward women that my father did," Kat said in a cool tone. "Which meant there were two locations for a woman, and that was the bedroom or the kitchen, preferably with a chain attached."

The two men working at the table raised their heads.

"In this day and age?" Cade shook his head. "Hell, I'd like to give him a good beating myself."

She stepped out of Badger's arms and started to pace. "What I don't know is why he would want me killed."

"Well, that's obvious," Paul said. "He's after those precious coins."

"How would he have known about them?"

"Was he not mentioned in the will?"

She shook her head. "No, we've had very little to do with him. He got out of jail a couple months ago. I honestly don't know where he's living or what he's doing."

"Blackmailing people," said the smaller man. "I know you guys want to keep us tied up so we can't attack you or something, and I understand all that, but I really got to take a leak bad."

She glanced at him in surprise, then at Badger, who was already untying him.

When the skinny kidnapper stood, he rubbed his wrists and said in a quiet voice, "I know you don't believe me, but I'm sorry for all the trouble."

Kat nodded. "Thanks. I just wish you hadn't kidnapped me in the first place. I'll have nightmares for the rest of my life now."

Badger led him away to the bathroom, keeping a steady hand on him.

She focused on Paul. "Do you know anybody name Teddy?"

He frowned, his thick bushy eyebrows almost meeting in the center as they furrowed. Then he shook his head. "No, I don't think so. Why?"

"That's my brother. His real name is Theodore, but he went by Teddy when he was a teen."

Erick spoke up. "We need to consider the fact that, if Teddy's an ex-con, and our guy here, his brother is an ex-con, it's quite possible the two met in prison." Erick got up from the table and walked over to Paul. "What's your friend's name?" He nodded with his head toward the bathroom.

"Bud. He goes by Bud."

"Okay, Paul, what's the relationship between you and

your brother?"

Paul stared at him, a hint of anger rippling across his face as he understood where the questioning was going. "Well, I would have called the authorities if I thought he'd set me up like this."

"When did you see him last?"

"Eight years maybe. He's been in jail since."

"What's his name?"

"Jonesy. Same last name. He went away for aggravated assault. I'm not expecting him out any time soon, but I haven't been keeping track."

Kat shook her head. "You said he changed when he came out the first time."

"He went in for armed robbery, and, when he got out, he wasn't the same man. He was uglier inside. The next time he committed a crime, he killed a man. He figured it was better to kill than to leave anyone alive to tell tales. But he got caught, and now he's in for murder."

"Wow, nice guy."

Just then Badger returned with Bud and sat him back down on the chair, tying his legs again. When Bud put his arms back to be tied up, Badger shook his head. "You can leave them free for the moment."

Bud's face lit up with a small murmur of "Thanks."

Badger stood in front of Paul. "Do you need a turn?"

Paul shook his head. "No, not yet."

"Found your brother," Erick said. "He's back East. I'm trying to get a history of any of the prison systems he may have been in, so we can match it with Kat's brother's prison history. If we can place them in the same penitentiary, I'll say we have a connection."

"I never would've thought my brother would do something like this." Kat shook her head. "I still can't believe it."

"How sure are you it was his voice on the phone?"

She winced. "Pretty damn sure. It's recognizable."

"Well, I hope you're also wrong about my brother," Paul said. "It's hard enough to deal with the things I've done, but, if my brother is gunning for me, that's a whole different story."

"Can you call him?" Badger asked.

"That's a good idea," Kat said in surprise. "Would he tell you what you want to know, or would he just laugh in your face?"

Paul stared at them and frowned. "I have no idea. I've never tried."

"He's allowed visitors, but he's a good three hours away, and that's flying time," Erick said, looking up from his laptop. "But you might be able to have a long-distance phone conversation."

Paul seemed to consider for a long moment and then shrugged. "What the hell. Why not? I need to get to the bottom of this somehow."

"Thank you," Kat said sincerely.

Badger looked at her and wondered at this switch—from being kidnapped to thanking her kidnappers. "Don't thank him yet. It doesn't mean we're getting anywhere."

"I'd say we've made progress very quickly," she said sharply. "Sure, it may not pan out to anything, but it could also end up getting us a whole lot further very quickly. We also now know Teddy's involved."

"What's his last name?"

"Same as mine," she said. "Greenwald. G-R-E-E-N-W-A-L-D."

"Theodore Greenwald was released on probation, living

in a halfway house here in Santa Fe, New Mexico."

Beside her, Badger said, "Bingo."

She pulled out a chair and sat down, her legs suddenly too weak to hold her up. "That's just shitty."

"Yeah, I'd say so. Sorry. Your family apparently sucks."

She pinched the bridge of her nose. "Isn't that the truth?" She glanced around. "I need coffee and food."

Cade put up a hand. "Count me in for coffee. A whole pot just for myself, please."

That startled a laugh out of her. She hopped to her feet again, happy to have something to do. She put on a pot of coffee and looked in her fridge. There wasn't a hell of a lot to work with. Especially if she were to feed this many people.

Cade glanced at her. "Unless you've got something against pizza, it's about the only way to feed us."

She peered around the fridge door at him. "Not exactly the healthiest food."

"Your stomach must be dying right now," he said in a droll tone. "Do you really want to go out with a spinach salad in your stomach?"

At that she really laughed. "Okay, you win."

"But what to put on the pizza? That's likely to cause an all-out fight," Cade said with a big grin.

She glanced at him. "Why?"

"Because Badger is a connoisseur of every take-out pizza around. He's got a very peculiar palate."

She grinned. "Badger, what do you want on your pizza?"

His eyes lit up. "I want a large just for myself, and I want it covered in bacon and olives."

She stared at him. "Anything else on it?"

His face went blank. "You mean other stuff goes on a pizza?"

She rolled her eyes and said to the guys, "You have the laptops. I don't know who to call."

Badger called out, "Pizza Palace. And you better get at least five large."

She stared at him. "What the hell? Who'll eat that much?"

He just stared back at her.

She groaned. When Erick read off the phone number, she dialed and ordered five large pizzas. She hung up and turned to the men. "Delivery in twenty-five."

They nodded absentmindedly.

The coffee had finished dripping. She poured herself a cup, then pulled out several other mugs. What about the two men tied up? Somehow she'd gone from being terrified to feeling sorry for them. She wasn't sure there was a happy ending for either of them. Particularly if they'd been blackmailed into doing this by her brother. That would really suck. On the other hand, if Paul had actually killed somebody, then how could she not want him to pay for his crime?

As she poured five more cups of coffee, not wanting to look too closely at why she was pouring coffee for the two kidnappers, she glanced out the window. "Badger?" she called out in a harsh whisper.

"What's up?" He came to her side.

She pointed out the window. "Somebody's skulking around my backyard."

Instantly the two men at the table got up and spread throughout the lower floor, slyly peering through windows. "What does your brother look like?"

"Small. Thin. He's about five nine. Always had a frail look. Women seemed to love it. I never quite understood the attraction myself."

"When you say frail, what do you mean? Slim, lean, pretty boy?"

"That wouldn't have been fun in prison," Cade said quietly from her right.

She stared at him. "I never considered that," she said in a low tone. "Maybe he took that time to bulk up. I don't know. I haven't seen him in forever."

"The guy skulking around out there didn't look familiar?"

"I didn't have a chance to look that closely. He's dressed in black pants, a dark sweater, and I think he had something over his head, but I don't know for sure. He disappeared into the bushes on the left side of the property."

Cade and Erick slipped outside via the garage door.

Badger spoke as he pushed her from the window. "Stay away from where you can be seen. Go sit down at the kitchen table."

She pulled a chair around in front of the two kidnappers, then placed two cups of coffee there for them.

Bud picked up a cup and smiled. "I really thank you for this. My hands are freezing after being tied up."

She glanced over at Badger and then back at Paul. "Do we let his hands loose?"

Badger walked over to stare down at Paul. "That's a good question. With his hands loose, he can cause a lot of damage." Badger opened his jacket so Paul could see the weapon in his shoulder holster.

Paul's face went ghostly white. He shook his head. "I'm no threat to you." He turned to Kat. "I wouldn't be here if it wasn't for your brother in the first place."

"*Maybe* her brother," Badger said. "We have to keep an

open mind here."

Paul shrugged. "Maybe, maybe not. But, if I get a chance, I will disappear, because the last thing I want to do is time for murder."

Kat could understand that.

"Let him have a cup of coffee while we see what the hell's going on outside. The man skulking around has the benefit of the encroaching darkness."

She turned to Badger. "We have to watch out for the pizza delivery guy. That'll add another element here that I don't really want to go sour."

"Nobody'll touch my pizza. Don't you worry about that."

She knew he was joking. But, at the same time, she wasn't sure just how effective a joke it really was. If something went wrong, it could just as easily be an innocent delivery guy who ended up dead.

BADGER DID A quick sweep through the house. He didn't want to leave the kidnappers alone, even tied they could have tricks up their sleeve. And once free it was just too easy for them to overpower Kat. That was the last thing that would happen on his watch. Every time he moved, he kept a close eye on Paul. His story sounded feasible, but Badger had heard more sob stories in his life than he'd believed were possible to exist. Everybody had an excuse; everybody had a reason for what they'd done. The fact was, they'd still done wrong. And that wasn't something he ever wanted to pit against Kat.

She sat across from the two men, the look on her face

sad, as if contemplating what had brought her brother to this point. Their uncle had been murdered. And the brother was after the coins—potentially. At least that was a viable motive. As Badger swept through the kitchen and came back on the other side of the living room, he asked Kat in a low voice, "Any chance your brother killed your uncle?"

She stiffened. Then, as she understood the ramifications of the question, she winced and said, "I don't know. It's possible. Like Paul's brother, Jackson, they start off with a certain crime, but it seems like jail changes them. The next crime is a little bit worse, and the next one is worse again. Just like Paul himself."

Instead of getting mad, Paul just nodded. He glanced at the coffee in front of him. "I know this probably isn't a great time, but I'd really like some of that coffee."

She went to stand up, but Badger said, "Don't move."

She shot him a look of resentment that made him smile.

Badger motioned at Bud.

He'd been sitting quite happily, sipping from his mug. At Badger's nod, he lifted Paul's cup and held it to his lips.

Paul took several big sips and then sat back, more on the happy side. "You make a mean cup of coffee, ma'am."

"I do indeed. Lots of late nights, studying. Lots of late nights, working."

Paul looked over at her. "What is it you do?"

"I guess you didn't feel the need to research your victims?"

At that he looked shame-faced and focused on the floor.

She shrugged. "I'm a prosthetic designer. I build arms and legs and hands for the men and women who have lost them, usually in war, but often in car accidents. Sometimes limbs wasted away from disease. Diabetes patients being a prime example."

The two men stared at her in surprise.

"And the three men helping me today all have prosthetics I've built. So they have a vested interest in keeping me alive."

Paul and Bud shared a glance and looked over at her. "I'm sorry. You do offer valuable services for people. I can't imagine the kind of work you do."

"I did twelve years of schooling to get this far. It's a little hard to imagine it all just being snuffed out because my brother is a piece of shit."

"Are you a doctor?"

She nodded. "Yes, and I'm an engineer. I was one of those smart teens." At the look on their faces she laughed. "Yeah, I was the one always in the library when everybody was out partying. Every time everybody took off from class to go smoke in the bathroom, I was the one studying and listening to the prof so I could get through the exams in half the time. I graduated at fifteen. Had my engineering degree before twenty, and I was a doctor before I hit twenty-six."

All the men just stared, their jaws slowly dropping.

She chuckled. "I do what I love because it gives me a chance to help these people. All the men here had their body parts blown off while they were in service to our country. It's a little hard for them to stomach guys who just break in and kidnap people for no reason."

"I know it's not much of a defense," Paul said, "but I *was* being blackmailed."

"Because you committed murder."

Badger winced. He'd been listening to the conversation, keeping track of everybody's facial expressions, looking for any sign of deceit, betrayal, something that would nudge him to a decision one way or another. But, so far, the men looked sincerely interested and possibly completely abashed at what they had done. Badger chuckled. "Yeah, when you picked a victim, you probably didn't realize how many people were here to support her. It's because of her I get to walk the way I do."

Both men glanced down at his legs. Bud said, "There's no way I would have known."

"That's because she does good work."

She rolled her eyes. "In many ways the men are better than they were originally. Their new legs have titanium and special gears to make the joints work properly. They are a cutting-edge design," she said with pride. "I'm really proud of the work I've been doing for them."

Badger could tell the kidnappers were desperate to see his leg. But he wasn't about to do a show-and-tell.

Paul spoke up. "Is that why Cade wears a glove?"

Badger nodded absentmindedly. "And you might think it's weaker. But I've got to tell you, it comes with a bionic punch."

Both of the men looked at each other again. Bud said, "Wow. That's really cool."

"It's really cool, but it takes a ton of work." Kat smiled. "Still, it's what I like to do."

"Then I'm really sorry we caused you any trouble," Paul said. "I'd like to get my hands on your brother, if he's the asshole yanking my chain."

"You might just get that chance."

The two kidnappers looked at Badger, but his gaze was caught on somebody skulking against the hedge. As he watched, Cade came up behind the intruder, threw a choke hold on him and dragged him back onto the property. "Cade just picked up our stalker."

Badger opened the garage door to let them in. Within seconds they had the struggling slim form of another male slammed down onto a chair, shifted to sit against the living room wall. Paul and his buddy were moved over to join him. Badger pulled the hood off his head. "Kat, come and take a look at this guy."

She gasped. "Teddy, what the hell are you doing?"

He glared at her and, in a hissing voice, said, "Hey, sis. Too bad you didn't die like you were supposed to."

"And why's that?"

"Because of course you inherited that shit from Uncle. He always told me that I would get them."

"I didn't even know he had them much less that I was getting them," she snapped. "How the hell did you know he had them?"

"Because Marge showed me. When she first married him. She's been telling me about them ever since." His tone was sarcastic, as if she already knew.

She stared at him. "They were married for what, three, four years?"

He shrugged. "Haven't you figured it out yet? Marge was Ethel's nurse. The whole time Aunt Ethel was dying, Marge was on the scene. As soon as Aunt Ethel died, Marge was right there. She learned about the coins a long time ago."

"How did you know her?"

"Because I was there at the hospital a lot more than you were. You were always at school or at a seminar or too damn busy."

"Are you telling me that you sat at the hospital with Marge?"

He shrugged. "I knew Marge's son. He's a druggie. And

he talks a lot. So I knew who made decisions in the hospital. When she married Uncle, I figured we would all do much better if he was dead."

She stared at him.

Badger could see how difficult this was for her. He walked over and sat beside her, his hand on her shoulder.

She swallowed hard and said, "Did you kill Uncle? Are you the one who broke into the house and shot him?"

Her brother sneered. "Why should I tell you anything?"

"Well, you're already up on charges for extortion and blackmail and perpetrating a murder for hire," Badger said calmly. "You might as well tell us the rest of it."

Instead the punk ass—who looked more like a kid who never grew up—turned and glared at Badger. "I don't have to tell you jack shit. I don't know who the hell you are. You're obviously trying to get cozy with my sister. Would figure she'd pick somebody like you. Big and brawny but no brains. She never could handle any competition in that area."

Beside Badger, Kat straightened in outrage. He squeezed her shoulder. "Sounds like your sister is one of those smart brainiacs, and maybe you're the one who couldn't handle the competition."

"I'm just as smart as she is. I just didn't care enough." He sneered and glanced around at the two men tied up. "What a bunch of losers."

"How is their situation any better than yours?" Kat asked. "You're my prisoner now too."

Just then a shot rang out, and the kitchen window right in front of Kat's head exploded.

CHAPTER 7

KAT SCREAMED AS she was slammed to the floor. Badger lay fully on top of her, his weapon out. Her brother had been tossed to the floor at the same time, and Erick had a knee to his back, and a weapon held against his head.

Then more shots followed. Each seemingly targeting something specific. One was aimed at her hot water heater in the kitchen, now flooding the floor. Another hit her fuse box on the other side of the kitchen door inside the garage and sent sparks flying, erupting in a small flash of fire that burned itself out quickly. She waited to see if her electricity went out. Two more shots passed through the same kitchen window facing her backyard to travel across the kitchen and into her living room, then exiting the big picture window there, which took down most of it in the process. Now the shooter could just walk in through the busted floor-to-ceiling window.

In a harsh voice Badger asked, "Who the hell is outside?"

Her brother laughed.

Badger leaned down and whispered in her ear. "I'll get up and go look. I want you to stay right here."

She nodded, and his weight came off her. She watched as he bolted across to the garage door, taking a closer look. Cade was already searching for the shooter through the windows, then followed Badger out to the garage. The two kidnappers in the chairs looked terrified. She crawled forward until she sat beside them on the floor.

Bud whispered, "What the hell did we get ourselves into?"

"I don't know, but it looks like its heading south very quickly," she said quietly. She studied the front window and their position. "I'm worried you guys are in the line of fire if the shooter fires from the front yard."

Bud looked at her. "If you don't mind, I'd like to lie sideways." And he dumped his chair backward. He lay on his back now, his legs up, then he rolled over once more, so he now lay sideways on the floor.

She glanced at Paul. "I'm not sure what to do with you. No matter which way I turn you, it'll hurt."

He said, "Don't worry about it. Sideways is best. I'd rather be hurt than be dead."

Together Erick and Kat lowered Paul's not-insubstantial weight until he was lying sideways on the floor, still tied to the chair.

She turned to see Erick tying up her brother. In the kitchen she pulled zip-ties from one of the drawers on the right. She crawled back, handing them to him.

He looked at them, and his face beamed. He put several together and tied Teddy's ankles and hands. She had also retrieved a dishcloth from one of the bottom drawers. She tossed it Erick's way, and he stuffed it in her brother's mouth.

Her brother gave her a glare, and she just shrugged. "You've already ruined my day. I really don't want you doing more damage."

With that Erick disappeared, just like the rest of his friends. A pair of kitchen scissors were on the counter beside her. She grabbed them. Did anyone ever have enough weapons in a situation like this? Unfortunately her brother saw her. His smirk said much about how effective he thought she would be. Still, as long as he didn't consider her a danger, he wasn't likely to do anything to call attention to her. It was just the kind of thing he did.

She held the scissors in her hands. If she got a chance, she had a special surprise she'd been trying out in her prosthetic. There was an advantage to no one knowing what she carried.

Five minutes passed with no change. Ten minutes passed with no change.

She turned to the two men lying on their sides. In a low tone she whispered, "Did either of you hear anything?"

"No," Paul muttered. "And I really hate the waiting part."

"Now I'm really worried about the pizza."

Paul looked at her incredulously.

"I meant the pizza delivery man," she corrected herself. "I don't give a shit about the pizza."

"I kind of do," Bud said in a light attempt at levity. "I have to admit to being pretty damn hungry myself."

Just then she heard a vehicle approach. "Shit."

What the hell should she do? Would the shooter let the pizza delivery guy walk up on his own? She crawled to the front door, stood and peered through the security peephole. Sure enough, it was the pizza delivery guy. At least one in a pizza uniform. Surely not the shooter in disguise. Not with Badger, Erick and Cade after him.

She sighed. She'd given her credit card over the phone already. Technically she was buying dinner for everyone. How the hell did that work? These assholes should be paying. But at least she didn't owe the delivery guy anything other than a tip. She checked her pockets and found a couple small bills.

When the doorbell rang, she opened the door, passed him the cash and grabbed the pizzas. She quickly shut the door and locked it behind her, then smirked at her missing picture window. She watched as he got in his vehicle and drove away.

When he was finally gone from sight, she let out a deep breath. "Okay, one less person we have to worry about."

Now she had to get to the kitchen safely with all the boxes. Crouched low, she avoided as many windows as possible. When she got to the table, she straightened enough to place the pizzas on its surface. And then she crept past her brother again to check on the two kidnappers.

"Okay, pizzas are here, but I really don't think we should be distracted by eating right now."

"Stay down and stay quiet," Bud said. "I think I hear someone."

She made her way to the door that led to the garage, careful not to slip in the water. All three tied-up men were tucked out of sight enough that, if the door opened, they couldn't be seen. She wanted to make sure she wasn't either. She sat on a pretty dry spot on the floor behind the door and waited. And waited. She pulled her phone from her pocket and sent a text. Just before she hit Send, she wondered if it would cause a kerfuffle. Did they all remember to turn their phones on Mute? Worried, she chewed on her bottom lip and then decided to hit Send after all. As soon as she pushed the button, she had second thoughts. But it was too late. Her phone responded almost instantly. It was Badger.

Stay inside and stay down. I'll be there in a few

minutes.

She frowned. But the smell of pizza was getting to her. Her stomach rumbled. And then she grinned. She was closest to the table. She crept over the few feet and snagged a box, dragging it back to where she sat against the wall. She opened it and picked up the largest piece. She sat there munching happily until the men returned.

She was three pieces down when they arrived. They were talking, so she assumed it was all good. However, all noise stopped when they took one look at her. She raised an eyebrow and took another bite. As soon as she swallowed, she said, "What was I supposed to do?"

The men looked at each other, snorted and walked over to the pizza.

"Does that mean it's safe now?" she asked.

"As safe as can be. The shooter's gone. I just wish I knew who the hell it was."

"Well, the good news is, we have my brother here. So either the shooter is an asshole who wanted *him* dead, or it was somebody who wanted me dead. In which case, my brother'll still be your best connection," she said cheerfully. "Can you sit these two guys back up?"

With a muttered exclamation, Badger reached down and helped right Paul again. Erick did the same for Bud. Cade, on the other hand, sat beside the open pizza box. She watched in awe as he placed one piece on top of the other, so he had two pieces in each hand, and started eating the stack on the left.

"Seriously? How can you even taste it that way?"

He looked at her, aggrieved. "It works great." And he took another huge bite.

A couple of minutes later all four pieces were gone.

That's when she realized five pizzas might not be enough. Now that it was safe, she put on a second pot of coffee. "Did anyone find the bullets?"

Cade said, "I've got three. The other two should be in the front yard somewhere."

"Are we calling the cops?"

Silence.

She groaned. "So, three of you guys are on the right side of the law. Three of you guys are on the wrong side of the law, and I'm stuck in the middle. I'd like my house back. I'd like my life back. And I want to know that these tied-up guys won't try to kill me again." She glared at everyone with her hands on her hips. "Doesn't that mean calling the cops?"

Badger shrugged. "It might be okay. Maybe call your detective. It's likely to be all connected."

"And what do I tell him?"

"Tell him you have a hell of a story, and you've got three guys tied up."

Bud piped up. "Or you could tell them just about two guys."

Paul snorted. "Yeah, better not mention Bud."

"Mentioning is one thing. Being charged is an entirely different thing," she said. "While I sympathize with your position, until we get to the bottom of this, none of us are safe. Have you considered that?"

Paul gave her a hard look. "I've definitely considered it. Have you considered the fact that whoever was shooting into your house may not have been after you, but might have been after us? We failed. He failed." He motioned toward Teddy on the floor, still tied up and glaring at them all. "Considering we all came here after you and didn't complete the job, this guy might have come to ensure none of us could talk and then to finish our job and kill you."

"I know," she said. "And that's not any help."

Just then Badger's phone went off again. He pulled it out, frowned and put it away.

"Who was that?"

He gave her a hard glance. "It's private."

She rolled her eyes. "Great timing for private conversations."

"Well, what am I supposed to tell them? *Sorry. I'm involved in a shoot-out?*" he asked sarcastically.

"Your private life is your own mess." She deliberately didn't look at any of their faces as she poured herself another cup of coffee. Badger's comment brought up unpleasant thoughts. Because of course he had a private life. For all she knew, he had a full-time girlfriend. Just because he acted like he was single didn't mean he was. Still, just because he acted like an asshole, didn't mean he was one either.

She groaned. "If I don't call the cops, how do I get any of these men out of my place? I'm not prepared to let my brother go free."

"Agreed," Erick said. "So call the detective whose card you have. If this is connected to your uncle's murder, then let's get to the bottom of that at the same time."

On that note she reached for her purse, pulled the detective's card back out and dialed. When a voice answered on the other end, she said, "Hi. My name is Dr. Kat Greenwald. I spoke to you before about my uncle's murder."

"Yes, I remember your name. I heard somebody reported a shooting around your area."

"I have three men tied up in my home," she said in a low tone. "Things just became really ugly."

"Don't let any of them go," he said, alarmed. "I'll be

there in five minutes. You stay safe until I get there. Do you hear me?"

"I hear you. And we were shot at from somebody else outside. We think the shooter is gone now, but I can't be too sure. So make sure you're careful when you approach."

There was silence for a long moment, and he said, "Okay, will do. I won't be alone either. Are you safe right now? Is somebody holding a gun on you?"

She thought about the knives she'd put in her ankle and back pocket and smiled. "No, I'm fine right now. And I have three men helping me. We've got the three other men tied up."

"Good enough. I'll be there in five."

BADGER TRIED TO step back when the police arrived. It was always hard to go from being a team leader in intense times back to being a subordinate. And no doubt law enforcement wanted to see all the general public in that manner. Badger knew he had failed when Kat shot him a look and said, "Down, boy."

He bristled. "What? I'm not doing anything."

"You look like a junkyard dog with an attitude."

"They kidnapped you, brought you home to hold you hostage in your own house, and you've been shot at. I think I have every reason to feel that way." Inside he marveled at her description. He was pretty sure his buddies would agree with it. He wasn't so sure he did. Was it insulting? Was it complimentary? *Junkyard dog* left a lot of room. Of course, when he looked at his face and the rest of him, it wasn't a bad description. He was pretty much a survivor of multiple wars. The thing was, he *had* survived, and he would hold on to that little tidbit of good news. Good news even if only long enough to find this latest asshole.

He inconspicuously pulled out his cell phone and checked for messages. He'd missed a call earlier from somebody with information. And that information he needed. He must slip away and make this call. He was sorry for all the hell now, but something else was breaking loose in his world. He'd waited two years for this. He wouldn't blow it now.

"Stay close to the cops. I'll just step outside and make a call."

She nodded almost absentmindedly.

He glanced around, caught sight of Erick and Cade, held up his phone and then slipped out the front door. It was a little quieter out front but not much. He walked to the end of the property on the sidewalk and returned his call.

The man that answered said, "I have news."

"I'm listening."

"It might cost you."

"Might? Looks to me like it's already cost me plenty."

There was a short silence on the other end. "True enough. All betrayal has a price."

"Sure, it does. Particularly for the victims."

With that the man on the other end swore.

Badger tried hard to tune his ears to see if he recognized the voice. But it wasn't familiar. "The guy who took the call left the navy soon afterward."

"In a rich and wealthy lifestyle?"

"No. A guilt-ridden one. Hit the bottle, lost his marriage, couldn't get another job, went homeless for a while, now he's working at a soup kitchen."

Badger lifted his gaze to stare at the house across the street. Kat's house was in typical suburbia. Simple block houses upon simple block houses, where everybody stuck to themselves, and nobody stuck out their neck for anyone. He shook his head. "Is he up to talking?"

"For a price. He did say something interesting."

"What's that?"

"He said his life changed and not in a good way. He's sorry for the troubles that you went through. But it's almost like you're better off than he ever was."

"Can't say I feel too sympathetic at the moment." Badger snorted. "If he did something to bring this upon me and my unit, he deserves every shitty thing life has available to throw at him."

"I hear you."

"How much do you want?" Badger calculated the money in his bank account. He didn't have a ton. But then what did he expect after a couple years of disability? Thankfully he'd saved all his money from his navy pay. But prosthetics from Kat had dipped into that nest egg recently. The navy covered much of the cost but not all.

"Ten thousand pounds."

"Is he in England?"

"He is."

"You aren't forthcoming with the information."

"You haven't said aye or nay to the agreement."

"Should be dollars," he said abruptly. Given the volatility of the American dollar and the British pound right now, it still wouldn't swing in his favor anytime soon.

"None of this should have happened in the first place. But it did. And it isn't in dollars. So make a choice."

Badger swore silently. "You getting paid for this?"

"Yeah," the middleman said drily. "Things haven't

changed that much. Except the prices went up, not down."

"As long as it's coming out of the ten thousand pounds, fine. Where and when?"

"Monday."

"Today's Friday. I can be there for Monday. Where?"

The caller mentioned an address in The East End of London. Badger stored away that information. "Time?"

"Just after noon. He also says come alone."

"Of course," Badger lied smoothly. "Just him and me."

"Better be. My neck is on the line for this one." And the man hung up.

Badger pocketed his phone as he turned to stare back at the broken window. His mind was already churning forward several steps. How the hell was he supposed to keep Kat safe and go to England? Then he grinned. There was a perfect solution. She would go with him.

On that thought he headed back inside.

She might fight him on it, but he knew his buddies would be right there with him. On the other hand, he could leave her with them. Although she wouldn't like that idea either. He grinned. He was actually looking forward to the upcoming argument. Kat didn't back down when he roared. Instead she reached out and clawed him one. He didn't have a problem with that. At least it meant she wasn't afraid of him.

There were certain people in this world who he wanted to be afraid. And the man he was meeting Monday was one of them. But Kat, never. The last thing he wanted was a cowed female in his bed. He wanted Kat, claws and all. And he wanted her damn fast.

He walked inside, a big smile on his face. "Change of plans."

CHAPTER 8

THE LOOK ON Badger's face made her suspicious. She studied the bright smile but could see the feral undertone to it. Whatever the phone call had been about had made him happy. Tension curled inside her now. She'd seen the same look earlier when they'd been shot at. When he'd been organizing an attack on the men after them. But this was different. And then she realized it had something to do with his other problem.

Her heart sank. Abruptly she said, "When are you leaving?"

He shot her a sideways glance, a hint of surprise.

She nodded. "I can see it on your face. Something's blown open."

"Something has blown *wide* open," he confirmed. "I have to go meet someone."

She shrugged, looking as if she didn't give a damn. But inside she did. Every step he took was one step closer to not coming back to her. Trouble was, he didn't even know she was here waiting.

She made yet another pot of coffee. She didn't know why she was constantly drinking the brew, but, if she couldn't have anything stronger, it seemed like the only solution for the moment.

Badger came up behind her. "Do you have a passport?"

She nodded. "Of course."

"Lots of people don't have passports," he said. "Or, if they do, they're not current."

"I planned on taking a vacation—when the business calmed down to the point I could actually walk away for a week or two—so I kept my passport current."

"Done much overseas travel?"

"No. Just down to Mexico and up to Canada. Once to England for a seminar."

"Long way for a seminar," he commented.

At the suspicious tone in his voice, she crossed her arms as the coffee dripped steadily behind her. "What does that mean?"

He shrugged and stepped back.

But she wasn't ready to let him off the hook. "What the hell's going on? Sometimes I say something, and it's like a box for you to check as you consider if I'm the bad guy or not, or maybe in cahoots with the bad guy?" She threw her arms wide open. "I hardly even know you. Right now, my hands are very full without you playing games." The cops walked into the kitchen at that point. She smiled at the detective. "Anything?"

"Nothing new," he admitted. "We've taken those three into custody. However, I need you to stay safe. At least until we can get this all tidied up and packed away."

"I've got an answer for that," Badger said quietly. "I have to leave for England. I'll take her with me. Get her out of the country while you round up her traitorous family."

She gasped and turned on him. "I can't just leave like that. I have a business, you know."

"The business needs to shut down for a few days," the detective said. "I know the work you do is important to everyone, but, if you're not around to do it any longer, you can't help anyone."

She glared at Badger, then at the detective. "How long?"

The detective thought about it and admitted, "If we have a good weekend, we might actually get this wrapped up before Monday. But I'd say at least give us until Wednesday. No guarantees even then."

Instead of agreeing, she spun on her heels and stormed off to the living room. Unfortunately she could still see and hear the men.

The detective looked at Badger and grinned. "That went well."

Badger raised his eyebrows. "What in all that do you think went well?"

"She didn't rant and scream at us," he said cheerfully. "Besides, five days in England is hardly a hardship."

She didn't know what Badger was up to, but she had no intention of going to England. Shutting down her company was not a cool idea. She had people who depended on her. People who needed her skills, just as Badger needed her skills. She wondered if she was overreacting. As she thought about it, she realized just how dangerous things could still be here.

And the weekend was coming up, but she didn't understand the England part. However, if she needed to disappear for a few days, England wasn't so bad. Jim could handle the office and could reschedule any appointments as necessary. Most people, if they understood what she'd been through, would give her a day or two of grace. As she stared out the window, she realized her complete about-face could also be a reaction to the letters, the kidnappers, her own bloody brother, someone shooting at her. And maybe a sign of stress and a sign that she *did* need to take a break. She turned to stare at Badger. "Why England?"

He stared at her for a long moment, shoved his hands in his pockets and rocked back slightly on his heels. "Because I'm going there."

"Why do I have to go where you're going?"

He shrugged. "So I can keep an eye on you."

"What about Cade and Erick? Are they going with you? Otherwise they could keep an eye on me here," she challenged. "For that matter, I have a cot in my office. I could just move in there for a few days."

She glanced around at the destruction of her house. "Considering my house has sustained damage, moving out for a few days wouldn't be a bad idea."

Cade and Erick moved closer to hear their conversation.

"That won't work," Erick said. "You won't get this damage fixed in a day or two."

She crossed her arms and glared at him. "I don't even know who to call to get this fixed." She waved her arm at the busted windows, the water standing in her kitchen, the scorch mark and smoke coming from the garage, not to mention the fingerprinting mess that had overtaken her house. "Does insurance cover this crap?"

All the men nodded. "Yes. You need to call the insurance company, file a claim and get estimates. But I think the cops are right. Even though they have picked up Teddy, we still don't know who else is behind this."

"So you agree with Badger that I should leave the country? Or that I should just leave the house?" She studied them carefully. She trusted these men. Of all those in front of her, she trusted Badger the most. But she couldn't get away from the feeling that he was up to something.

"Definitely out of town would be better. I'd hate to see you move into your office because anybody who can't find you here will automatically go there," Erick said. "And I'd hate to leave Jim there alone to be tortured for information."

She couldn't help the gasp escaping her mouth. She stared at Erick. "Are you serious?"

Badger stepped forward and grabbed her by the shoulders, giving her a small shake. "You were kidnapped outside your office, held hostage in your own house. Now shot at. At what point do you not see how serious this is?"

She bowed her head. "Surely I can go somewhere else. I could take my laptop and my work, go to a hotel or something."

"Or you could go to England," Cade suggested. "Get out of the country, see some new sights, take your work if you want because I can see that's something you'll never really be parted from. And let Badger keep an eye on you."

She glared at him. "I know *you'll* keep an eye on Badger." She leaned forward until she was glaring at him eye to eye. "You know he's up to something. You know England is part of his deal. And, if it's part of his deal, it's dangerous as hell. Why would I want to go from one danger to another danger?"

Cade opened his mouth to answer, then slammed it shut. He frowned as if considering her words and turned to look at Badger. "Why will you be in England?"

In a low tone Badger said, "I'm meeting somebody who accepted the orders that changed our route that day."

Instantly the air charged with interest as the men took a moment to digest the information.

Erick let out a long, slow whistle. "Are you serious?" He looked over at Cade. "I think we should all go."

Kat shook her head. "I think I should stay behind, deal with the insurance company and get my house fixed up," she said firmly.

The detective stepped back to her. "No. I don't want you here."

"Will you give me protection then?" she snapped.

He grinned. "I think these three can protect you just fine."

She glared at the detective. "What you mean is, if we run into trouble in England, it's not your headache."

Badger looked briefly hurt and then considered the options. "At least in England, people will have trouble finding you. Here it's pretty obvious where you would be."

She shook her head. "I could hide out in any number of hotels, any number of states, cities, towns. No one will find me."

"Yes, they will," the detective said firmly. "I bet these three know exactly how to travel without leaving any tracks *unless* they want to be found. You, on the other hand, will go to the bank, withdraw a bunch of cash, not take quite enough, so you'll use your credit card at various stops to order food, pay for a hotel, and that credit card will get traced, and you'll have people knocking on your door within hours."

She frowned. "I could take out a larger amount of cash."

"And how will you get to wherever it is you're planning on going? These people already have your license plate number. So now you either need to rent a vehicle—you can't do that without posting a driver's license—or you'll have to take a bus or fly, in which case you have to use your credit card to get a flight."

"If I go to England, my passport will be used to get a

flight," she snapped in frustration. "Look. I don't have a problem going to England. It's just a hell of a long way to go for no particular reason. Plus it seems to me that I'm going from the fat into the fire. Because, what you don't know is, these guys have their own shit to deal with."

The detective looked at the three men, studying their hard glances and heavy military look, even though it had been two years since they were active. She stared at them too, and her shoulders sagged because she knew exactly what the detective saw. Three very capable men who knew exactly what to do in times of trouble. And they probably had a ton more experience in this kind of shit than even he did.

She raised both hands in agitated surrender. "Okay, fine." She hesitated. "Still, I can't leave my house wide open like this. I've got a handyman I've used before, and Jim has a set of keys to my house. Jim can oversee getting these windows boarded up in the meantime." She glared specifically at Badger. "But I'm taking work with me, and I'm staying in the hotel. I'm not going to any clandestine meetings you guys set up."

Badger grinned. "No problem. How do you feel about fish and chips? There's a lovely spot by the docks."

She shook her head. "I don't care where we go," she said tiredly. "I'm not sure I'll sleep anyway. So sure, let's just walk London until I drop." She glanced around her house, full of forensic techs and uniformed cops. She could see the neighbors gathering outside. "It'll hardly be kept quiet here, will it?"

"Nope. We can nicely leak to the newspaper that you've left town for a few days, and your office is closed. Give your staff some time off, make sure your office is secured and go away for a while. Leave us to do our job," the detective answered. He turned toward some men waiting to speak with him. "I have to go. You've got my card. Send me a text with an update and an email giving me the details on your flights and where you're staying." With that last note he turned and walked off.

She fingered the card. "I guess I can do that."

Badger shook his head. "That's the last thing we'll do."

She looked up, startled. "But he just told us to."

Badger leaned forward and whispered, "I don't give a crap's ass what he said. If we're trying to hide you, no way will we send an email giving some asshole all the directions where you can be found." He straightened up and looked at his watch. "You've got a few minutes to grab yourself a bag, some work or whatever it is you need to take with you from here. Then we'll swing by your office. You can pick up anything else there, check to make sure everything's locked down, and we're out of here."

She looked from one man to the other. "All four of us?"

"Likely more," Erick snapped. "Seven of us were involved. Seven of us got blown up that day, who are still alive. That means seven of us have a vested interest in our future."

She frowned. "How safe is it for me to be around you guys?"

"Safe enough," Erick said with a big smile. "We'd never let anything happen to you, Doc."

She knew she could believe him. But also that they couldn't be everywhere all the time. Shit happened. She only had to look at what was left of her house to see that. "Then I'm heading upstairs to pack." She slowly maneuvered her way toward the stairs, pulling out her phone to call her handyman and Jim.

The detective stopped her and asked where she was going.

"Upstairs to pack a bag."

He motioned to a police officer. "Go up with her. Wait until she's packed and then escort her back down again."

She frowned, not particularly liking a police escort to her bedroom, but at least it was a policewoman. Plus Cade and Erick too. Wow. Three people to watch her pack her undies and things. She called Jim first, caught him at home and spoke to him. Then she reached her handyman as well. What were the odds of that happening at any other time?

Upstairs she pulled out her smallest suitcase and a carry-on bag and quickly packed up clothes for a long weekend. The trouble was, she didn't know what she would need.

As she hemmed and hawed in front of the closet, Cade said, "Pack something nice. We'll take you out for dinner a couple times."

She turned to stare at him and frowned. "How nice?"

He grinned. "I'd love to see you in those red high heels."

She glanced down at the stilettos he pointed at and shook her head. "Hell no. I don't have room to pack that kind of stuff." Neither was she prepared to go out dancing at this stage of the game.

However, she had no reason not to take a couple nice outfits. She carefully packed a few skirts and pairs of pants that would go with anything, and a couple really dressy blouses, and a completely backless dress she could roll up into a tight ball. But it was black and it needed black shoes. She bent down into the back of her closet and pulled out not the red stilettos but a pair of black ones with slightly lower heels, put them in a bag in her suitcase and then walked to her dresser and emptied out what she needed. When she zipped up both her bags, Erick grabbed them and carried them down for her.

She stood in the living room and stared at the organized chaos inside and the police Crime Scene: DO NOT CROSS tape going up outside. "I never thought to see this here."

"And let's hope it never happens again." Badger stood at her side. "Are you ready?"

She turned to look at him, saw he had a hand out to her. There was something much more meaningful about that hand than just him helping her out to the vehicle. She knew it, but she couldn't stop herself from reaching back, placing her long slim fingers in his big mitt. She wasn't far off when she had called him a junkyard dog. The good thing about junkyard dogs was that they were trained to look after their junkyards. And, for whatever reason, she'd been included in the things he was looking after.

BADGER DIDN'T HAVE much time to make preparations. But with Erick and Cade beside him, it went much faster.

After picking up the luggage and hustling Kat into Erick's truck, Erick drove them all to Kat's car where the kidnappers had left it, a block or two from her house. Erick and Cade followed as Badger drove her to her office, where she quickly went in and made some phone calls. All the while, Badger stood watch. Then she gathered some work, set the alarm and stepped out of her office.

She stood in front of the closed door for a long moment, then turned to look at him. "I'll be coming back, won't I?"

His heart lurched. He reached out a hand again, grasping hers. "Absolutely. I promise."

Of course it was a foolish promise. But what he really

meant was, he would do everything within his physical means to get her back to work. He didn't expect London to be a problem, but he knew staying here would definitely be an issue. The best thing for her was to get out of town for a few days.

Leading the way, he moved her downstairs and back to her car, waving to Erick and Cade, who then took off. As soon as he turned on the engine to her car, he said, "We'll go to my place so I can grab some clothes. Then we're heading out to the airport."

She gave a start of surprise. "So fast?"

He nodded as he pulled her car into traffic. "We're flying overnight."

For this time of day, traffic was light. That didn't mean the wrong person wasn't out there waiting for them. The last thing he wanted was to get picked off by a sniper as they moved toward getting answers to his own mystery.

At his place, he parked in the driveway and hopped out. He waited as she got out and stopped beside her car, staring at his home. In a quiet voice he said, "It was my parents'."

She studied the massive Victorian style house built in the forties. "This is incredible."

"It is. It's also a ton of maintenance and renovations. There seems to be no end of those."

He led her through the garage door into the kitchen area, knowing what she saw for the first time was something he'd grown accustomed to. The exterior of the house might be Victorian, but the inside was contemporary, modern and as high efficiency as anything she'd ever see anywhere. But then he loved to cook. He also hated inefficiency. There was a massive island counter in the center, with a stove, sink and cutting boards built in.

She wandered around, her fingers trailing across the quartz countertop, and whispered, "Wow."

"Do you want to see the rest of the house?"

She nodded. "I so do."

He gave her a quick tour of the downstairs. The huge vaulted living room couldn't be seen from the outside because of the dormers in the front; it appeared to be a second-floor hallway across. She stared up three stories, her neck cranked back. "Holy crap."

At the very top were stained-glass windows and sky-lights. With the light shining through right now, colors danced across the hardwood floors. "This is incredible."

He nodded. "My father and I did a lot of the work to-gether."

As if sensing the change in his tone, she asked quietly, "What happened to your parents?"

He smiled. "They were the typical homebodies. They were killed in a car accident. T-boned in an intersection. And no the guy was never caught." His smile turned reminiscent. "They'd been together fifty years. They were both eighteen when they married. I was a late baby for them. They just couldn't stand to be apart. And in that way, I'm glad they went together." He moved Kat toward a huge spiral staircase done in hardwood. "I haven't got treads on these, so watch your step."

"It seems almost sacrilegious to walk up here with shoes on."

"You better keep them on, at least until I get a carpet runner or put inlays here that would stop you from slip-ping."

She followed as he ran lightly up the stairs. On the sec-ond floor he stopped and took a left. The left side of the house was the master suite. As he opened the big double doors, she gasped again. He smiled. He didn't show his place to very many people. Not many understood. They all thought he was rich as Moses when they did see the place. The fact was, it was paid off within twenty years, and he and his father had spent all Badger's childhood fixing it up. When he had gone into the military, his dad had continued to work on the house. It was a labor of love for him and his mom. And for Badger. Some of his best memories were tied up in this house. He never intended to sell it. Ever.

He walked over to his walk-in closet and heard her call out, "Is that like a changing room or a walk-in closet?"

He laughed. "Both. My dad started to make changes, but my mom came in and said it was nowhere near big enough. Next thing we knew, the second bedroom upstairs was converted into this. But it has separate entrances."

She walked inside. "You have an island in your closet?"

His laughter rippled out. "I do indeed." He opened drawers to show her ties, socks, underwear, everything below the hanging suits, jackets, winter coats. All his clothing pretty well filled one side.

She turned and saw the bulk of the other side was completely empty. "Well, that's a good sign."

He stopped and frowned at her. "Why is that?"

"Obviously you're not living with anybody at the moment."

"My coonhound, Dotty. She's being looked after by the neighbors right now. But, no, I've never lived with anybody in this house except my parents," he said shortly. "The military is hell on relationships. I got close to the altar a couple times, but I never made it."

She nodded. "Me too. I've been a bridesmaid and a maid

of honor but never the bride."

He chuckled. "Third time's the charm then."

She shrugged. "Not that I believe in superstition or things running in threes," she said, "but I don't have anybody in my life right now either."

"Yes, you do." He pulled out a large duffle bag, laid it open on top of the island and started sorting through his closet.

He finally became aware of the odd silence behind him. He spun around and looked at her. She stood with her hands on her hips, her legs in a wide-apart stance and a mutinous look on her face. "Who is supposedly in my life?"

He loved that about her. The punchy attitude, the aggressiveness that really was just a kitten trying to sharpen her claws. He went back to packing his dufflebag. "Me. At least that's the cover we're traveling under. We're engaged to be married in a few months. You just refuse to set a date."

She gasped.

He started to laugh. He'd known she wouldn't appreciate that cover.

He turned to face her only to get a towel thrown at his face. He looked at it. "No, we should be good with the towels. We'll be at the hotel after all." And he tossed it back at her.

She just glared at him, letting the towel fall to the floor.

He walked around, picked up the towel, tossed it into the laundry basket. "We have to have some reason for the way we're traveling," he said in a reasonable tone. "Besides, you don't want people to think you have a bodyguard, do you?"

That seemed to settle her down, if the stiffness loosening in her back and her hands dropping to her side meant what they should mean. "Fine, but you could have at least asked me about it."

"What was there to ask?" He closed the duffle bag and stopped to study his closet once more. "I have to go downstairs to the office, collect a few more things." He grabbed his bag and walked out to the hall.

"What's up the stairs?"

He glanced over at her and smiled. "We have about five minutes if you want to take a quick look." At her eager nod, he dropped his bag and took a quick right, up the next flight of stairs.

She followed. When she got up there, she didn't even gasp, she just stared in wonder. The space was mostly empty, except for some discreet and casual sitting arrangements with big windows and the skylight above. All the hardwood floors gleamed. "This is a social area?"

"A big-screen TV is against that far end wall. I come up here to watch TV or have friends over for drinks. But I always thought it would be a great place for kids to play."

"Or office space," she said in excitement. "Wow, this is incredibly beautiful."

He shrugged. "It is, but it's something I'm quite used to. I was literally born in this house. Every beautiful childhood memory I have is wrapped up into the hardwood floors." He touched one of the huge wood beams. "We left the original structure, but there's not a whole lot else that's original."

He turned back to the staircase. "Come on. Time to go."

When she reached his side, he took it slower going down the stairs. He wanted to ensure she didn't fall. Lots of people didn't bother, but he wanted a carpet runner or something to give a little bit of traction.

On the main floor he headed into his office. She was a

few steps behind him. He went behind the door, pulled a picture off the wall and opened the safe there.

She had walked straight to the French doors that opened up to the gardens behind the house. "Can I open the doors?"

"Sure." He pulled out his passport, money, contact book and a few other documents he thought he might need. He walked to the desk, packed up his laptop and stood, wondering if he was forgetting anything.

Then he realized she was standing outside on the patio, staring and crowing in delight. He loved that she enjoyed his house so much. It was a very classy home. And he'd seen all kinds of different reactions from people over the years. It never grew old. He stepped out, looked at the beautiful pool, hot tub, gardens and patio. They went with the large backyard. "It's time to go."

She nodded. "Okay. I'm coming. But, when we get back home, I want to swim in that pool."

Images of her in a bikini filled his mind. He took a deep breath, willing all the heat to dial back down again. In a low voice he said, "Now that would be perfect."

She glanced at him and smiled. "You've got to make sure nobody marries you just for your house," she teased.

"That thought has occurred to me." With her back inside, he closed the double doors, set the security alarm and walked her out to the garage. "We've got just enough time to make it to the airport."

"What about Erick and Cade?"

"They're already there." He led the way outside. "I'll move your car into the garage, and we'll take my truck."

Once loaded up, he turned on the truck engine, pulled it back out of his driveway and mentally said goodbye to the one piece of his life that had always been there for him—his home. He watched as she twisted to keep the house in sight as they drove away.

"You're very blessed," she said. "I can't imagine having a place like that as a home. But I think I'm more jealous of the fact that you actually grew up in it. Watched it grow and change with you. Worked on it with your father and created those memories that are still very special. In comparison, my life was cold, empty, full of change because we moved a lot, full of houses that weren't homes and friendships that were fleeting. You've not only managed to hang on to your childhood home but to the friends who were there with you the whole time."

"How do you know I've had friendships since way back when?"

She laughed. "Because you're the kind of guy who would."

She settled into the truck seat and was silent for the rest of the journey.

CHAPTER 9

WALKING OUT OF the airport in London, Kat studied the gray skies and drizzling rain and shook her head. "I've been in this country once before. It was exactly the same weather. There was such a cold then that it seemed to penetrate the bones with this never-ending dampness. I was at the conference the better part of a whole week. Never got a chance to get out of the hotel. So I saw the weather through the plane or the hotel windows and in the cab ride from the airport to the hotel and back again to the airport. It never changed. The view was always incredibly depressing."

Badger took her elbow and motioned her toward a taxi.

"Don't we want to rent a vehicle?"

"No. Erick already has one."

She slid into the back of the taxi.

Twenty minutes later, with lots of honking and traffic noises, vehicles going every which way, she murmured, "Now this is why I live in a small town."

He laughed. "Exactly. Unless you happen to love a busy metropolis, London isn't the place for you."

"Well, it is if I'm a tourist," she said with a laugh. "I don't know what exactly we are doing here. And, if the weather ever changes, it might be nice to get out."

"We will get out a lot," he promised. "Whether the weather changes or not."

"I didn't bring anything for rain," she said worriedly. "How could I have not brought a raincoat?"

"Not to worry. We'll make out just fine."

When the taxi pulled up in front of a large hotel, he helped her out, paid the fare and hooked her arm through his. "Remember, we're in a relationship. We're engaged, about to get married in the next few months." His voice was low, only for her ears. "We're here on a business trip."

"What business is it exactly?"

He gave her a sideways glance and a big grin. "*Your* business."

She raised an eyebrow, her mind spinning to look for reasons why she would be here. And then she remembered a couple of the profs and speakers who had been at the conference last year. "I was definitely trying to connect with a couple men. They did tell me, whenever I was in town, to contact them. One even has a fantastic lab. I'd really like to see it." Her voice picked up with enthusiasm. She couldn't help it. It was her specialty. "If we can fit that in, then I will consider this trip very worthwhile."

"Where is he?"

She frowned. "I'll have to check my email. A vet here who does prosthetics. I know it's not a system that works well for humans yet, but I was thinking that, maybe in your case …"

She felt his sharp glance but didn't explain. How could she explain that currently prosthetics were held on by suction and proper fit? But then he knew that. The vet, however, was actually putting steel rods into the bones on animals so legs could be clipped on permanently. And, if something broke, then a new leg could be put on through the permanent locking system. She had no idea how that would work for humans, but, because Badger had lost his leg so high up, in a way it would be a much better option for him. But she didn't think the practice would be approved in the US anytime soon. And finding a doctor to do that kind of surgery would be difficult. Caught up in her musing, she didn't realize they were already at the reception area, and he was signing the paperwork for their room. Two key cards were handed over, and a bellhop discreetly picked up their luggage, putting it on a cart, and led them toward an elevator.

Upstairs on the fourth floor, the door was opened into a large bedroom with double queen beds. She noted the sleeping arrangement with half a thought, wondering if he'd done that on purpose. In a way she wished there was only one bed. She knew exactly where she wanted this guy. And that was beside her at night, hopefully caught in a passionate embrace.

While he dealt with the bellhop, she walked to the window for a look outside. Traffic streamed below. Other buildings stood everywhere she looked. Another hotel was across the street, with more windows, apartments and hotel rooms staring directly at her. She shook her head but loved the size of the bridges up and down the Thames River.

Hearing the door close behind her, she turned to see Badger walking into the main room. They'd flown overnight, but, with the time change, it was late afternoon already.

He stopped and looked at both beds. "Left or right?"

"The one by the window," she said quietly. "One room?"

"You won't be alone at any time until your nightmare is over."

There was an autocratic tone to his voice. As if prepared for an argument and wanting to head it off first. She didn't plan to argue. But it was a sign of concern that he had set it up this way. In a quiet tone, she said, "Thank you."

Surprise lit his gaze.

Just then a knock came at the door. She raised her eyebrows. "Did the bellhop forget something?"

He shook his head. "It's Erick and Cade."

He opened the door and let the two men in. They entered with big grins flashing, just in jeans and T-shirts. They looked as comfortable here as they had back home. Her glance went from one to the other and then to a third man who had entered the room.

She studied his face for a moment and realized she'd seen a photograph of him in her medical files. "Talon?"

The man stared at her, his eyes like obsidian, and asked in a low voice, "How do you know my name?"

She crossed her arms and tapped her fingers, thinking about the details of the medical report. She knew he had one prosthetic below his left knee. He had more leg left than most. He also had a plate in his right leg and back injuries she wouldn't wish on anybody. And then there was his missing arm ...

"I'm Kat, prosthetic designer." She smiled. "And your file crossed my desk. With your photo."

He raised one eyebrow. "I didn't know that was included. And?"

"I sent an affirmative back to your doctor."

At that, the room lightened considerably. He grinned, made his way through the men and shook her hand. "Much obliged, ma'am." He studied her for a long moment. "You're not exactly what I was expecting."

She grinned. "I get that a lot."

But she could see he was still hesitant. "Yes, I'm a prosthetic engineer. Yes, I'm a doctor. Yes, I can help you. I don't know how your stumps and the scar tissue are at this point, and whether you're ready for some of the more developed prototypes, but, as soon as I can get back home again"—she turned to glare at Badger—"you can come to my office and we'll start the testing."

He nodded and, in a smooth drawl, said, "Even more reason to keep you alive then."

She laughed. "In that case, I am glad to have you on board," she said drily. "But honestly I think the only person in trouble here will be Badger himself. My troubles are at home."

At that, the men sat to discuss the little information they had gathered. As she listened, she realized they really didn't know much. They had a name. They had an address. They'd already picked up the money they were paying somebody to give them answers on a directive that had been given and then changed. She listened quietly, standing by the window, watching the four of them. So very similar in many ways and yet so very different. They were all extremely fit. There was an air of quiet confidence but also an urgency about each one, as if they needed to solve this problem before they could move on.

The last thing she wanted was for any of them to get hurt. And yet she could see how she could do so much to make their lives easier. Talon's left arm was a very simple unit. She knew he had shoulder straps, and the manipulation of his fingers were extremely slow. The articulated joints were old school. She had a much better one at home.

Finally she realized one of the men was speaking to her.

"Kat?"

She took her gaze away from Talon's arm to look at Badger. "Yes?"

"You ready for dinner?"

She nodded. "Just waiting for you grannies to be done with your gossip."

Erick laughed. "Doc, I forgot you had such a great sense of humor."

"Hell, I didn't even know she had one," Cade said with a big grin.

"I don't," she said in a dry tone. "There's just something about having been shot at, kidnapped and now hiding away in London while you guys plan your revenge that makes this all seem extremely supersecret spy stuff and way over the top. In other words, humor helps me get through it."

Badger smiled. "Good. Whatever works. Let's eat."

BADGER WATCHED AS Kat led the way to the lobby. All the men positioned themselves around her, determined to keep her safe. He wasn't sure who would be a target in England. He was hoping nobody. He doubted her troubles had carried over to this country, but that didn't mean his troubles weren't waiting for them here—although a simple meeting or a few questions shouldn't be an issue, at least he hoped not. But then they were carrying some money. And that always led to problems. Whether he liked it or not, a lot of people would kill for ten thousand pounds.

As they walked out onto the street, his phone rang. He pulled it out to see it was his contact. "Hello?"

"He wants to change the time. He's getting nervous. He

wants the money so he can leave the country."

"When does he want to meet?"

"Tomorrow morning?"

Badger glanced at his friends. They were studying his face, half listening in on the conversation. "That's possible. We're in England now."

"His first choice was tonight. It's only four o'clock. Do you want to do it now then? I'd have to get back to him and confirm."

Badger's instinct was to say yes. The sooner, the better, but he worried about taking Kat with them. "See if you can make it happen." He hung up and quickly told the others about the change in schedule.

Kat frowned at him. "Well, I'm not about to get sent back up to my room," she said. "We can all go and meet this guy and then go out for dinner."

Badger shook his head. "The informant was extremely clear. I have to go alone."

She protested. "No. That's too dangerous."

Erick spoke up. "There's a pub around the corner from the address where you'll meet him. The rest of us can eat and wait for you there."

"That still doesn't protect his back," Kat exclaimed. "We don't know anything about this guy. He could be waiting with a shotgun."

Erick looked at her in surprise.

Badger just laughed. "I'm expecting something along that line."

"Why?"

"Because he wants money from me. He's hoping that whatever information he has is worth enough that I'll leave it behind."

"But that's the deal, isn't it?" she asked. "He gives you the information he has, whether it's good or bad, and you pay the money, whether you're happy or not."

"Sure, if he has any information. It could all be a ruse."

"A ruse for what? Is somebody after you?"

"Not necessarily. But I'm asking questions. If somebody is behind our accident, they will not be happy to hear I'm reopening the investigation."

Her back stiffened, and she shoved her fists into her pockets.

Mannerisms he was coming to understand told of her stubbornness. She balked at the idea of him going alone, whereas he couldn't wait for this meeting, as this guy had information he wanted, and he wanted it now. His phone rang again.

"Twenty minutes." And the phone line went dead.

He checked his watch, pulled up the address on his GPS and said, "We'll probably take a taxi."

Erick shook his head. "No. No trails. I've got a car. Let's go."

They piled into his vehicle and were on the road within seven minutes. Badger knew they'd make it in time, but he'd like to be a few minutes early.

The drive was only seven minutes as well. As they pulled up outside the pub, Erick pointed to the corner building. "He's in one of the flats up in that building."

With a hard look at Kat, Badger said, "You stay with Erick and Cade. Sit down, grab a beer, order some dinner. I'll be back before you know it. Talon will keep watch for me." Badger took off, walking past the apartment building, scoping it out. When he realized it was clear, he turned back and entered through the front door. There was no panel to call up to say he was here. There was just an open door. That in itself set his back up. But he was in England, in one of the poorer areas. Even if there had been a call-up center, it probably wouldn't have worked. Instead of taking the elevator, he raced up the stairs.

He was five minutes early, and that was a good thing. He walked down the hall to the right number. He froze. The door was open ever-so-slightly. He put an ear to the door and heard someone moving around inside. He knocked on the door hard. It opened, surprising him. A stranger stared at him nervously.

"Come in, come in." The stranger stuck his head out in the hall, checking to make sure nobody had followed Badger. "You sure you're alone?"

Badger walked all the way into the small living room, seeing an old couch with sagging springs, windows with no curtains and the mattress on the floor. It didn't look like a quick shack up but that the man had lived here for a few years at least. He turned to face him. "Yes. I'm alone." No lie. Talon was on watch but well out of sight.

Badger studied the stranger—a man in his early forties, a lock of brown hair over his face, a thin lanky frame and skin too sallow to be healthy. The man was trembling, but Badger didn't think it was from nervousness. Drugs? A disease? He wasn't sure, but the man looked like he was only a few steps away from death. Badger stared at him straight on. "I believe you have some information for me."

"Do you have the money?"

Badger pulled out the pack he'd brought with him and opened the top so the man could see inside. Badger didn't bother asking for his name because, even if he'd been given one, it wouldn't be the real one. But he memorized the man's face so he could confirm any information coming from him. "Now what do you know?"

The man's voice was thin, reedy, but he seemed sure as he spoke. "I was running dispatch that day. You'd all been given your orders, checking out the territory, looking for any of the insurgents who might still be in the hills." He took a deep breath as if struggling, then shrugged. "I received a call saying that one of the roads was bad. Intel was that antitank IEDs were on that road."

"And which road was that?"

"The road where three of the vehicles were supposed to go."

"And who called it in?"

"Corporal Shipley."

Badger frowned. He didn't know that name. "Who made the decision to reroute us on the other road?"

He shrugged. "I don't remember. I passed on the information to my superior, and I received a change of instructions that I sent right out again."

"And you're sure you gave him the right road?"

The man nodded. "After the truck was blown up, I went back through the information and confirmed it. We'd been told the road you were on was bad, and your truck needed to take the route I gave you."

"Just my truck?"

He nodded. "The other two were sent on different routes."

"Our truck was sent on a specific route. A route that took us over an antitank land mine."

The man nodded. "The problem is, when we went to double-check the information, we couldn't find a Corporal Shipley."

Inside Badger didn't know if he should scream for joy or punch out this asshole. It was what he'd suspected. Somebody had fed them bogus information. But somehow that information had to have been cleared. And it was this guy who did it.

"How hard did you look?" Badger's voice was hard, steely.

The other man seemed to shrink inside himself. Yet, at the same time, it was as if something fell off his shoulders.

"Did you get paid for passing on false intel?"

The man backed away, shaking his head. "No, no. I didn't."

But, for the first time, his tone made Badger doubt him. Badger studied him for a long moment. "I don't believe you. You knew the information was bad, but you sent it anyway."

The other man winced and sagged into the closest seat. The couch made a groaning sound as it took his weight. "I didn't know it was bad, honest. But what I didn't do was I didn't check Corporal Shipley's tag. I should have checked to make sure the information was good. And later, when I did, I realized there was no Corporal Shipley."

"Shit."

The informant nodded. "How do you think I've felt these last two years? It's because of me that you got blown up." He looked at Badger, his eyes red-rimmed, drug induced, hazy. "I'm so sorry."

What the hell was Badger supposed to say to that? Seven men badly injured, their careers completely wiped out and Mouse, ... poor Mouse. He stared at the man with contempt. "Was anything ever done to follow-up?"

The informant shook his head. "No, because I had already passed it on as solid intel. After the incident, my superiors assumed I had either received bad intel, mixed up the routes, or you just hit an antitank land mine that nobody knew about."

In the eyes of the military, theirs was just one more accident in a long string of accidents. There was no way to tell if the intel was bad or good—except there was no Corporal Shipley in the navy. He let his breath out slowly. "Were there any background noises? Other voices?"

The informant looked up and nodded. "Yes. But I couldn't hear very much. Voices in the background. Honestly it sounded like a truck full of guys."

"Any chance you made a mistake about the information?"

He shook his head. "No, it was taped."

Badger's interest piqued. "Do you have a copy of that tape?"

The man stared at him and then slowly nodded. "I do. I erased it at the base when I realized what had happened. It's garbled too. Another reason why the military decided to look the other way and make an excuse that it was an accident. But I taped a copy first. It's not great, but it's still something."

"I want it," Badger said in a harsh voice. "Where is it?"

The man dug into his sweatpants pocket, pulled out a USB key and held it up. "But I want the money first."

Badger walked over to the small table in front of the window, plunked down the pack and took out the money. He placed it on the table and said, "And now I want that key."

The man hopped up and raced over, his hands eagerly reaching for the money.

Crack.

The hole that appeared in the window was followed by a hole in the informant's forehead. The look of stunned surprise crossed his face. It all happened too fast.

His body crumpled to the floor.

Badger ducked, quickly grabbing the money to shove it back into his bag. On his hands he crawled over to the informant. He took a picture of his face, snatched the key out of his hand, stuffed it in his own pocket and crawled to the door. He didn't know how long before the police would arrive, but he had to make sure he wasn't here when they did.

With a gloved hand, he opened the door and stepped out into the hallway. He took the first fire exit and bolted downstairs.

He went out the back door to the alley and around the block. When he entered the pub seconds later, he watched the relief cross Kat's face and realized just how much she was starting to care. Damn good thing. Yet every step he took down this road, he realized he might never come back. However, something about his relationship with Kat was a lifeline for him. If anybody would stop him from dying in this quest of his, it would be her.

CHAPTER 10

H E SLID INTO the empty seat. Kat leaned over, kissed him quickly on the cheek and whispered, "What the hell happened?"

He gave her a sharp look. "What makes you think something happened?"

She gave a half snort and settled into her chair.

He glanced at the others and said in a louder voice, "Did you order for me?"

Just then the waitress delivered platters of fish and chips. He smiled. "How very British." A beer arrived at the table in front of him.

Kat watched him glance around the room as if to see if anyone could overhear. Apparently satisfied, he leaned forward and said, "The informant is no longer."

Kat stiffened. She stared at him in horror.

He rolled his eyes. "Not by my hand."

She sighed and relaxed slightly.

Erick asked, "Was he dead when you got there?"

Badger shook his head. Kat listened as he explained what happened, but inside she was too shocked. She'd warned him that this was a dangerous route. That the man was shot right in front of him was unbelievable. And yet, after what she'd been through, how could she be surprised. Maybe the surprise was that she'd spent the first thirty-something years of her life untouched by this kind of violence. And now there just didn't seem to be any end to it. As much as she was shaking and could hardly pick up her glass of beer, Badger appeared to be completely calm.

Erick said in a low tone, "Did you see anyone?"

Badger shook his head and nodded to the street across from the pub. "The shot came from that corner building. Fourth floor would be the most likely."

"Should you go look? Where's Talon?" Kat asked. She couldn't believe what she was asking. "And what about the police?"

"I haven't heard any sirens," Cade said. "Keep in mind this is a slum area. Violence isn't abnormal here."

"I left the door as I found it, which was a hair open. If nothing else, now somebody is likely to go in and case the place and see if he's got anything to steal. Maybe Talon saw something, but I doubt it."

She couldn't let that happen. "It's not fair to the inform-ant. I don't want to consider his body sitting there in that room for days going unnoticed."

"It won't," Badger said. "I have a contact here. I'll get the word to the police."

With that she had to be happy. Still the fish and chips she'd been looking forward to before didn't look quite so appetizing now. She couldn't believe he'd come close to getting shot. She raised her gaze, studying him. "Was the bullet meant for him?"

He looked at her with respect. "Good question. And, yes ..." He lifted his finger and as if imitating a bullet, drove it directly into his forehead.

She swallowed hard. "You're lucky. You could have been next."

"I could have been," he said cheerfully. "But they never got a second chance. It would have been better for them if they'd taken me out first and then him."

There was silence for the next few minutes as everyone digested what had happened. She watched as Badger plowed through his food. His appetite seemed unnatural. Wrong somehow. He had just watched a man die in front of him. Then she remembered grabbing the pizza when she was hiding at her own house. Was that any different? Was that a reaction to the stress? Or was it the instinct of knowing she would need the food for fuel?

As she stared down at her plate, she realized Badger was being the smart one.

She attacked the fish on her plate with a zero-minded focus that had her inhaling the rest of her food in seconds. When she sat back, she saw all three men staring at her in surprise. With her mouth still full, she shrugged, embarrassed at her actions. When she finally swallowed, she said, "I realized I needed the food. It didn't matter whether I wanted it or not, but, since we don't know what's coming, it was fuel."

All three looked at her with added respect and nodded. Just then Talon walked in, spoke to the waitress and joined them.

Badger looked at him, questioning. Talon shook his head.

"Too bad. It still feels wrong," Kat said.

"Death should always be wrong," Badger said quietly. "It doesn't matter who or how."

She wrapped her arms around herself, wishing the chill would go away. They'd only just arrived, and yet they'd already accomplished the intent of what they'd come for.

And, in many ways, had gotten themselves in peril and something so much worse. "Are we going home now?"

"We'll return to the hotel and dig some more."

She nodded and sipped her beer, while the men finished their platefuls. Talon received his food and dug in. Afterward they paid for the meal, got in the car and drove back to the hotel. The whole time she felt like she was being watched. She didn't think she really was; it was more a case of nervousness. She'd always lived on the right side of the law, had a certain amount of respect for those in that position. But these men ... Not that they were on the wrong side of the law, but they understood it in so many different ways than she did.

She listened as the men discussed the night's events but came up with nothing new.

Back in her room she lay down, tucking the pillow under her head. It wasn't that she was tired, but a few minutes time out from the world was not a bad thing.

Badger grabbed the blanket across the bed and flung it over her shoulders, covering her up. "If you want to sleep, go ahead."

She shook her head. "I don't think I can. I'm just not sure what's happening right now."

"The others are coming in soon. We'll have a powwow."

When Talon walked in, he carried a small device. He turned it on and walked the room. She watched in surprise, but, when he was done, he pocketed the device as if nothing was unusual about his actions.

She sat up slowly. "Did you just check for bugging devices?"

"I did," he said cheerfully. "The good news is, there aren't any."

"Why did you think you needed to check?"

"Because chances are the reason the informant was shot was so he couldn't speak to Badger."

"But he was shot *after* speaking to Badger."

"Did the shooter know that? And maybe he was also sending a warning to Badger—to stop or we'll stop you permanently."

She flung back down on the bed and stared up at the ceiling. "This isn't the world I'm used to."

"And you don't want to get used to it. It's a world very few of us live in. The public, by and large, is safe. Law-abiding citizens go about their day, working their eight-hour shifts, raising a family and enjoying weekends. Not all of us have to skulk in the shadows all the time."

"Did any of you consider you no longer have to?" She kept her voice even, calm, but a part of her felt these men needed to be reminded they were no longer active SEALs.

Yes, she understood there was no such thing as an ex-SEAL. But these guys were no longer on missions either. They were retired. On medical leave. Whatever it was they wanted to call it to make themselves feel better. It was important for them to understand this wasn't the way it necessarily had to be.

The men just stared at her. Not one said a word. She brought up her hands, palms up. "Fine, just ignore me then. But you could choose peace and quiet for a lifestyle now."

"Like you did?" Erick asked, his tone full of interest. But there was also no humor.

She gazed at him. "Watch it, or I might just stick something in your prosthetic that backfires."

"Would that be backfire, like a gun that misfires, or something that backfires, like a stink bomb exploding all over me so I embarrass myself in public?"

Her jaw dropped as she stared at him. "Wow. And here I thought I was being creative with the prosthetics. Maybe I should just go full-on crazy with yours."

He sat down on the bed beside her, a big grin on his face. "Please do. I don't know if you can make them wild-ass crazy designs too, but I'd sure like to have something original and just for me."

She smiled. "Stone's girlfriend has been doing a lot of design work. She's done some pretty amazing ones for prosthetics."

"I've heard that," Erick said. "But that's more of the pretty design work after the structural work is done. Honestly, the kind of stuff you do is pretty awesome, but I think you could get a little more futuristic looking in your designs."

She rolled her eyes. "I have a bunch of designs. But I haven't exactly worked out the engineering yet."

"Let's see." He picked up her laptop and brought it to her. "If you've got them, I'd love to take a look."

"Is this an attempt to keep my mind off what just happened?"

He shot her an innocent look. "I don't know what you are talking about."

"Right." She turned on her laptop and waited for it to boot up.

The other men sat on the other bed or stood around with their heads together.

She nodded toward them. "I really don't want to know the details. But I don't want you making plans with my life that I don't have any say in."

"Don't worry, Doc. We will do everything we can to

keep you safe."

"*Safe* isn't necessarily the answer either." With her laptop up and running, she brought up her folder on design work. There was a lot she could do. If she was at home right now, she'd be going over these designs anyway. It was one of the things she had fun with. Her heart was very much caught up in what people could do. Bionics was a world all on its own. And she really wanted to be at the leading edge of that.

She just wasn't sure that she'd be able to.

She opened the folder, set it up as a slide show and turned it so Erick could take a look, then hit Start. He sat in rapt attention as the slide show went through the images she'd saved. These were hand sketches, some done in digital programs, others done on paper and scanned in. As she watched his face, her heart warmed. These were the men she was working toward helping.

It was one thing to give them a practical way to live their life; it was another to give them something they were proud to wear. And would fight over for a better design. After a long moment she realized the other men had come to cluster around Erick to see the designs themselves. When it ran through one time, Badger restarted it. She listened to their comments as they discussed the various adjustments that would work for them.

"Is that a pocket? Like a place to hide a knife?"

"It's a knife sheath. Along this back piece is a space that would hold a 9 mm Glock," she said quietly. "I was thinking of the law enforcement men who I work with."

They whistled and laughed like little boys as each design came out, from hands to arms to legs. Even a couple for back support.

Talon looked at it. "Surely those steel plates haven't been

implanted in anybody, have they?"

She glanced at the one he referred to and shook her head. "No, that's a plate for around the waist, rods driven down through the legs for a particular patient I'm working with. His pelvis and hips aren't strong enough to support him. We're looking at ways to give him some stability at the same time." It was an extremely advanced design and would require surgery. She shook her head. "It's not very practical yet at this stage. But I can't stop thinking about how to make his life better."

When the room fell silent, she turned to look up at them. Every one of the men stared at her with a different expression on his face. She frowned. "What's with the looks?"

"I don't think you realize how special you are, Doc," Cade said with a smile.

Erick patted her hand. "Anytime you feel you want to create something completely off the wall for my problem, please just do it."

She laughed. "None of this is cheap," she admitted. "If I could find a way to 3-D print the pieces and have it survive you guys longer than a couple weeks, I would do it in a heartbeat. Certainly 3-D printing works for some things. But the metals are a whole different problem. The vet I wanted to visit over here implants permanent rods coming out of his patient's legs that he uses as a base to attach simple joints and legs. Artificial knees, artificial hips, artificial legs, feet, ankle joints. There are cats running around with just steel pins for stumps. You put a rubber stopper on the end so they have traction, and it works very well." She glanced at Badger. "If I thought I could get a surgeon to take on your case, I'd want to see something like that for you."

The others all turned to look at Badger. He crossed his arms and glared at her. "I don't like the idea of surgery."

"No, but how do you like the idea of losing your prosthetic because your stump is on the short side? What if you had permanent metal implants coming out of the bone that could attach to prosthetics? You wouldn't have to worry about them falling off, coming loose, scarring up your flesh, nothing."

He frowned at her. "Is that possible?"

She shook her head. "Not in the human world. But it certainly is in the animal world."

He looked interested in spite of himself. "But we'd need a gifted surgeon to come on board?"

"And lots and lots of tests, yes," she said with a smile. "I imagine the surgery would be minor, but we'd have to make sure your body wouldn't reject the metal."

"It's an interesting thought though."

"It's actually the future. Not that the legs have to be something that can come off and on, but you want them to be something you can switch out for a new design, like running blades." She shrugged. "Something with a better knee. Something you can lie down with and put a lot of weight on for workouts. It's hard to imagine all the different uses. It's just a matter of how much design work we can do, and that's individual to each body. Because each joint is different—each man's weight, tone, muscle, and what's actually left for me to work with. There's nerve damage, muscle damage, tendon damage." She shrugged again. "No simple answers. Just a lot of research."

"But it sounds like you're the one to do it."

"Oh, I'm certainly the one who would like to do it." She laughed, the sound freeing and happy, grateful for the change of conversation. "That's what I really love to do."

BADGER WAITED ON a phone call. Several of them actually. But, with this new twist of events, he'd like to get Kat back home as soon as possible. The trouble was, her house was still a mess. And they had come all this way. It seemed a shame if she didn't get a chance to do something for herself.

Just then his phone rang. He stepped closer to the door for a bit of privacy.

"You didn't have to kill him," The middleman said to Badger.

"I didn't." Badger quickly explained. Then there was silence on the other end.

Badger didn't know who this middleman was, but, if Badger wanted to procure more information, this go-to guy had to know that the informants were safe from Badger.

"Did you see the shooter?" the middleman asked Badger.

"No. I wish I had. It was dark out. I'm not even sure the cops know about it yet."

"Maybe that's for the best. He was living pretty well underground for a long time."

"I still need more information."

The man snorted. "Not if you leave a trail of dead bodies."

He knew the man was about to hang up, so Badger cried out, "Wait ..."

"What?"

"There's money in it for you too."

"I'm not up for bullets in the back."

"I didn't have anything to do with it. Obviously somebody knew he was meeting me."

"That could only come from you."

Badger shook his head. He knew the informant himself could've told somebody and so could this guy on the phone. But information brokers would be putting their own lives on the line if they didn't keep secrets. "He gave me a recording."

"Good. At least you got something out of the deal." The man's voice was full of disgust. "But I'm not sure anybody else will be too helpful."

"That's not true. People always like to talk."

"I don't know where else to get anything for you. I'll have to think about it carefully."

"Good. Think about it. Just know I didn't have anything to do with this. And, if somebody is tying up loose ends, we need to catch him too."

"Good luck with that." And the phone went dead.

Badger glanced at everyone sitting on both beds, now staring at him. He shrugged and put away his phone. "He's not sure he'll help out anymore."

"Why not?" Kat asked. "You didn't shoot that man."

"No, but it means somebody else out there knows what I'm after. Knows these bread crumbs will lead us to the truth. And that's something they'll try to stop."

She slowly got up off the bed and walked toward Badger. "So, I'm asking again, where do we go from here? Can you find out anything else while we're here? Because that was a hell of a long trip for a five-minute meeting."

"That happens sometimes." But still, he did have a few other things he could do. "Maybe the guys will take you to the vet's tomorrow. I think I'll do some research."

"What kind of research?"

He glanced down at her and smiled. "What's the matter?

You worried about me?" he teased.

She put her hands on her hips. "I have a vested interest in your leg."

He leaned closer and whispered, "Only my leg?" And watched in delight as color rolled wildly up her cheeks.

She shot him a disgusted look, turned and walked away.

He glanced down at his watch. "It's late. Let's regroup in the morning."

With that, he escorted the other men out. They talked in the hallway for a few moments, decided that nobody needed to stay on watch because there was no personal danger. They would reconvene at six in the morning.

When he stepped back into the room and locked the door behind him, she was in the bathroom. He opened his case and took out his shaving gear. His mind was still full of what had happened earlier.

If there'd been anything he could have done to have stopped it ...

Had the murder been planned, and Badger was an incidental witness? What were the chances the killer knew Badger would meet with this guy? Had the informant told somebody? Did he have a partner? Somebody who would steal the money? But, in that case, why not shoot Badger instead of the informant? Something about that whole deal just stank.

He stripped down to his boxers and waited for her to come out of the bathroom. In the meantime, he brought up his laptop and entered some data. He knew Stone would be willing to help. But he might need a little more information. Badger made a phone call to the informant's apartment manager, caught the night clerk and asked for the identity of the man in the apartment with that number.

"Why do you want to know?" the bored guy at the end of the phone asked.

"I think he lost his wallet," Badger said in a quiet voice. "I wanted to return it to him."

"If he lost his wallet, then his ID is in there."

"Yeah, but there's a couple IDs. I need to know which one is the real one."

"That's funny. He would have a bunch of IDs. That guy is a drug addict and an alcoholic. He was former navy, retired—apparently out of life."

"Name?" he prompted.

"Ben. Ben Chambers."

The phone went dead with a *click*. It was late where Badger was, but it wasn't late in the US. He dialed Mason. When a woman's voice answered, he said, "Tesla? It's Badger."

"Badger? Where are you?"

"I'm in England. I'm kind of in a spot. Any chance I can talk to Mason?"

"He's right here. Hold on."

"Badger, what's up? And how are you doing these days? I haven't heard from you in a long time."

"Yeah, there's a reason for that. I need information on former navy personnel."

"What kind of information?" Mason asked cautiously. "And do I know the name?"

"He's the one who changed the orders that rerouted the truck I was in that blew up. He took the intel from a Corporal Shipley. Only when he went to check into the information after the fact, he found out there was no Corporal Shipley."

"What?"

Badger could almost see Mason sitting down, a shocked look on his face. "Yeah." And he filled him in on what he'd learned so far.

"And he was shot right in front of you?"

"Yeah. I'm not sure where to go from here."

There was silence for a long moment, then Mason said, "I can see if Ben Chambers or Corporal Shipley are in the system. I may not be able to get any more information than that."

"I'd appreciate it if you could do that much. The information I've just found out does confirm we were directed onto that road with the antitank mines. That means it was a deliberate attempt to sabotage the run. Seven people injured and one dead, Mason. How is that even acceptable to *not* have anybody looking into it?"

"From the brass's point of view, there isn't enough to go with. But you know, if you find evidence, then they'll back you up."

Badger could hear Tesla in the background talking.

"Tesla says Ben Chambers left the navy two years ago. No reason given. Medical was normal and performance was average."

Shit. "So maybe because of this incident he guilted out."

"Maybe. Remember though this is all evidence. Once we get to the bottom of it all, the brass will have to look into this."

"I'm not even sure I know that anymore. I hope so. But I have to find the evidence first. I do have a recording ..."

"Can you send it me to?"

"I can. Do you have any equipment that can work with it?"

Mason laughed. "I'm sure Tesla would be on that in a

heartbeat."

In the background Badger could hear Tesla call out, "Sounds like new toys for me to play with. I'm always happy to help out. You know that."

Badger smiled. "I'd appreciate it if she would. I'm downloading the audio file onto my laptop now. I'll send you the secure transcription."

"I will get back to you if anything's there. And you stay safe. Just because the informant took the hit, doesn't mean there isn't a second bullet for you. You never actually showed up again for him to target, did you?"

"No. I booked it out of there, went out the back and disappeared down the street. We never saw the shooter leave the building either."

"Okay, this can go both ways. So you make sure you watch your back as well."

"Will do." He ended the call at the same time Kat came out of the bathroom.

She smiled. "The bathroom is all yours."

He smiled back, his fingers busy on the keyboard. "As soon as I transfer this audio file." As he hit Send, her scent drifted across his nose. He lifted his head and said, "Wow, I don't know what you just used, whether it's on your hair or your face or what, but it's nice."

She blushed. "It's my night cream."

He studied her face and shrugged. "I'm a guy, and I don't know anything about that stuff, but, from here, it has a lovely scent." He let his gaze drift over her long body, now in some kind of a camisole and shorts, and saw her own prosthetic. An ivory-colored piece, both feminine looking and functional. It was beautiful, and her shorts hugged the curves of her thighs and wrapped lovingly around her buttocks. He could feel his body tighten in response.

He slapped the laptop closed, swung his legs over the edge of the bed and got up. He swore as his leg shifted underneath him. He reached for the wall to stabilize himself. And then without looking at her, headed to the bathroom with his shaving gear. That was one thing about not spending nights with women. They didn't have to see his weaknesses at times when he couldn't hide them. He carefully took off the prosthetic and unwrapped the cotton layer. And winced. His leg was not happy.

He stared at the puffy flesh in dismay. He'd been doing his damnedest to not let anyone know how bad it was. Kat would have a fit if she found out. *Just let me get through this, and let us get home, everybody safe and sound, and then I'll go back to crutches for a few days. Give this leg the break it needs.*

He studied the stump, wondering if it was even possible to do what she said with the steel implants used in cats. And whether his doctors would okay it. Experimental surgery was never their way. Malpractice suits being the headache they were, often doctors were afraid to go out of their comfort zone. Badger would have to talk to the orthopedic surgeon and see what he had to say. Badger had looked online about the veterinarian she'd talked about, had watched several other videos of what he did. At least it was enough to give Badger a rudimentary understanding of what she wished they could do for him. And Badger agreed it would be great. But the type of spikes they were putting in those animals were small, whereas, to hold him in place, those would have to be fairly substantial. Still, it was something to contemplate.

But not now. He had shit to do first.

CHAPTER 11

K AT WOKE UP the next morning to voices at the door. She bolted upright to see Badger fully dressed, talking to someone outside in the hall. She checked her watch, seeing it was 6:10. Surprisingly she'd fallen asleep right away while Badger was in the shower. She had wanted to ask him about his leg, but he was stubborn, and the junkyard dog was always sitting at the edge whenever she came close to the subject.

She brushed her hair off her face and called out, "I'm awake. You don't need to be quiet."

Badger turned around to look at her. "Do you mind if they come in?"

She shook her head, shifted so she leaned against the headboard and pulled her sheet up across her chest. When Erick came in with a cup of coffee for her, she beamed. "Wow, this is special treatment. I can't remember the last time I got coffee in bed."

The guys shook their heads. "You're sleeping with the wrong man then," Erick said with a grin and a nod toward the bed Badger had obviously slept in.

She smiled up at him. "No, I don't think so. Just so you know, we're not sleeping together." She accepted the cup of coffee from him, placing it on the night table beside her. "So what did you guys find out?"

Talon gave her an innocent look. "What makes you think we were looking for anything?"

She snorted. "Of course you were. You wanted to make sure Badger wasn't shot and to catch the guy who shot the informant."

Talon shrugged. "I went back to the apartment building. The police crime scene tape was up, so they have obviously found the body. I didn't try to go in. None of the neighbors seem to know anything. Or, if they do, they're not talking."

She stared at him in disbelief. "Were you expecting anyone to talk to at this hour? Won't they be pissed off at being woken up?"

"Some were just coming home from working the night shift," he said with a smirk. As if the nature of that work was questionable.

"In which case they probably don't even know what happened yet. What about the guy at the desk or the manager or the maintenance guy?"

"Checked with whoever I could find. Nobody knows anything."

"I, on the other hand," Erick said, "contacted my buddy at the police station. He said the information was slammed shut. He wanted to know how I knew about it."

"What did you say?" Badger asked, a frown creasing his forehead.

"I told him that we'd been in the pub, and we heard something weird, but we didn't see anything."

She stared at him and laughed. "So, give him a little bit of the truth to keep him happy, just not enough to make him question it."

He nodded, giving her that knowing smile. "Exactly."

THEY WERE SEATED at the back of the hotel restaurant, finishing their late breakfast. Badger wanted to cut Kat loose for the day so he could go to the apartment building and the room the shooter had to have been in. He knew there was a good chance the cops would be on-site. But there was also a good chance they'd already moved on. He doubted a drug-addicted, washed-out guy like his informant would garner a whole lot of police investigation hours. Sure, they did their job, but it was an area with a high crime rate. Unless they got any decent leads, there was no way to close the case.

Not only was Kat not having anything to do with his idea, neither were the guys.

Talon was being most adamant. "We stick together."

Badger glared at him. "Why now? We've always gone off in teams of one or two, gathering intel before."

Talon shrugged. "But we currently have somebody we're protecting at the same time."

"Exactly. No way I want to add her into the mix," Badger said. "She's already got enough headaches. This could put her in more danger."

"So we don't mix the two," Talon said. "Let me go. Nobody here knows me. Nobody back home from her situation knows me. I'll scope out the apartment. You take her to the vet clinic she wants to go to."

Badger fought it, but the voice of reason finally prevailed. As a last parting shot, he said, "What about your logic that we needed to stick together?"

"That was to stop you from going off on your own," Talon said with a big grin.

Badger checked his watch. "We'll check in on the hour."

He glanced at Kat. "How long until your meeting?"

"It's at eleven. He doesn't have much time to spare. If I had longer, I'd probably stay and watch as he did surgeries. But I'm not sure that invitation is in the offing."

The men nodded. Talon said, "I have my own set of wheels, so we'll see how it goes."

He went to stand, and Cade stood with him. Talon looked at him in surprise. Cade just gave him a blank look back. Badger smirked. "Two at a time."

Talon shrugged, as if not caring either way, and walked out. Badger turned to Erick and Kat. "It's about an hour's drive once we get out of the city, maybe a little more. And at least fifteen minutes to get out of the city."

She nodded. "In that case, I have time for another cup of coffee."

He motioned for the waitress who came over with the coffeepot. She refilled everyone's cups.

Once she was out of earshot, Kat said in a low tone, "Will they be okay?"

Badger nodded. "Chances are they'll be back here before we're even gone."

She gave him a frown that made him smile. She asked him, "Is there anything you can do that's effective while we're here?"

He shrugged. "We're looking for another informant. People are analyzing the audio file. The names in question are being researched. It's all going on in the background. That doesn't mean there's anything in particular we can do about it yet."

"Before we head out, I want to check in with Jim."

He nodded. "In that case, as soon as you're done with your coffee, we'll go back up to the hotel room, and you can use the landline there."

She thought about that. "No, it's the wrong time for Jim. I'll wait until this afternoon. Do we have time for more coffee?"

He glanced at his watch. "Well, if we don't linger, you'll be fine." He watched as she dumped extra cream into her coffee and drank it down in several big gulps. "I didn't mean you had to inhale it."

She grinned. "I'd inject it if I could."

With Erick laughing out loud, the three made their way back to their rooms. As they approached Kat and Badger's room, Badger held up a hand. Erick slid against the wall, coming up to the side of the door. Badger motioned Kat behind him flat against the wall and whispered, "The door is open."

He heard her sucked-in breath but didn't have time to reassure her. Inside they could hear someone moving around.

Erick motioned with three fingers, dropped one, then another, and casually walked inside. "Hey, what are you doing in here?"

With a sharp word to Kat to "Stay here," Badger raced inside after him.

Erick was in the middle of a fight with a small wiry man. Badger wrapped his arms around the man's neck, put him in a chokehold, tossed him on the bed and thrust his knee into the center of his shoulder blades. With a look at Erick, he said, "Get Kat in here."

But Kat was already at the door, slamming it shut. "*Kat, stay here. Kat, come in.* I do have a brain, you know? I can understand when it's dangerous and when I need to get the hell out of the hallway because you guys are making a ruckus in the room."

Badger glared at her. But he was relieved to see she wasn't upset. If anything, she looked energized at this turn of events.

She walked over and stared at the man and shrugged. "I don't know who he is. Do you guys?"

Badger shook his head.

Erick checked the man's pockets. He pulled out a wallet and flipped it open. "Well, look at this." He held up an MI6 ID card. "Jonas Halpern."

Badger whistled a low-key sharp sound that filled the room. He slowly eased back, checking for weapons, and found two, one in a shoulder holster and one in Jonas's boot. With both of those removed, Badger sat back and let the man sit up. "So what the hell does MI6 have to do with searching my room illegally?"

"What the hell are you doing over here in the first place with your cohorts?" Jonas snapped. "And I'll have my ID back please."

Erick was busy taking a photo of it. Once he was happy with that, he returned it. "We'd like an explanation, Jonas."

Jonas shrugged. "You guys arrive. Some guy is dead. Calls are made. Your name never quite gets mentioned, and then I start getting phone calls from friends on the US side. It's enough to peak my interest. So I came calling."

Badger laughed. "Close but not close enough. MI6 should never have been alerted. This was a simple police case. And your friends from the USA don't have any reason to suspect any of us in any wrongdoing."

"No, but I did receive a call from an informant, saying you were asking questions that would get some people shot." Jonas gave Badger a hard grin and said, "And look at that. Somebody got shot."

Badger stared at him for a long moment. His heart sank. "What the hell does MI6 have to do with this?"

"Maybe nothing. But I have informants all around the world. And, when something goes down in my backyard, I'd like to know what it's about." His gaze went from the two men to Kat. "Particularly when I run her name and find out several suspicious deaths and multiple shootings surround her."

Kat glared. "I don't know who you think you are," she snapped, "but none of those cases had anything to do with me."

Jonas snickered. "And yet you were kidnapped and shot at?"

She shoved her hands in her pockets. "I don't like you."

His response came quickly. "I don't give a shit if you do or if you don't. I want an explanation as to why you're over here."

"Not until we find out who it is you talked to in the US," Badger said quietly. "And just in case you think I don't have anything on you, you're wrong. I have lots of connections in MI6 myself. You entered our room illegally and were doing a full-bore search *illegally*. Without suspicion, without cause."

"It depends if I find any of your DNA in a room where a man was shot last night," the agent said coolly. "But let's cut the crap. You're over here to do a job. I don't know what the job is. But, so far, one man is dead. I don't want any more dead."

"Agreed. Sorry about the dead man," Badger said in a cool tone.

"Now you see? That apology would work better if I didn't believe you were there or at least somewhere around there."

"As we already gave a statement that we were at the pub around the corner, obviously we were there," Erick said in exasperation. "There's an easy answer for all of us. But it means the two of you need to stop bristling at each other so we can talk."

Jonas gave a quick nod. "You first. Tell me what the hell is going on."

Erick and Badger exchanged hard glances, then Badger said, "We had reason to believe an informant had intel regarding a directive that was changed when we were on an active mission. That change in orders ended up with seven men blown to hell and one man killed."

Jonas's gaze sharpened as he digested that information. "And what information did you find here?"

"The information that caused the change in orders came from somebody who doesn't exist," Badger said quietly. "And I received an audio file of that conversation last night."

"Did you shoot the informant?"

Badger shook his head. "No. But he was shot in front of me from across the road. Another apartment building."

"Damn." Jonas scratched the back of his head. "I really wish you'd keep your shit on your side of the ocean."

"It would have saved us time and money if our inform-ant wasn't over here."

"Was the information good?"

"He's the one who took down the new intel and sup-plied it to our superiors without checking and confirming it." Badger sighed. "To give him a little bit of leeway on that lack of diligence—don't forget we weren't expecting a particular problem, and we were all out in the field—when he got the information, he told his superiors the orders were changed, our route was changed, and we were blown up by an antitank land mine."

Jonas's gaze narrowed as he studied Badger and then Erick. "You were in the truck that was blown up?"

Badger nodded. "There were eight of us, and one died in the accident."

"Did the audio file have anything worthwhile on it?"

"We're waiting for somebody to get back to us on that."

"How did you find the informant?"

Badger gave him a steely smile. "The usual way. Another informant. And money. Lots of money."

They all sat in silence for a long moment.

"I'm sorry for your friend," Jonas said. "And particularly if you think this was done on purpose."

"I always believed it was done on purpose," Badger said. "But I could never find any proof. How does one accept intel from somebody who doesn't exist?"

"Yeah. It means the intel is something you don't want to be traced back to you." Jonas nodded. "I would have preferred that you brought this to me in the first place, but I can understand why you didn't. The thing is, I can't have you shooting up any more of our citizens." He held up a hand, stopping Badger from protesting once again. "You may not have done the shooting, but, because of your arrival, the man is dead."

"Agreed." Erick stepped forward. "Did you guys find any forensic evidence from the shooter?"

Jonas shook his head. "No, not yet. And I highly doubt there will be any. It was a sniper rifle. Barely caused any damage to the glass. No shell casings. No forensics that we could find at this time. Testing is still ongoing with carpet strands and a few hairs. But it's a rent-by-the-week flophouse, so there'll be hair and other forensics. None of it'll necessarily pinpoint who our shooter was. In fact, I'm sure he went in completely gloved and suited up in order to not leave anything in the room itself."

Badger felt a hand slide into his. He glanced down to see Kat standing beside him, her fingers laced with his. "Do you have any cameras on the area?"

Jonas glanced at her, but, instead of answering her question, he asked her one of his own. "What is this going on in your world?"

She winced. "It looks like my brother met somebody in jail and made a pact to kill my uncle for some rare coins. Only I inherited them, so they decided to kill me."

He stared at her for a long moment and then shook his head, pointing from Badger to Kat. "Wow, you two deserve each other."

Badger squeezed her fingers and chuckled. "You might think so, based on that," he said, but his tone didn't show the same lightheartedness as his laughter. "But know this, neither one of us would choose these circumstances. We just want to have a decent life again."

"You're obviously not too badly hurt ..." Jonas studied him and then Erick. "Although I imagine antitank land mines means you didn't get off lightly."

"We all lost limbs, muscle function, incurred some major internal damage. We're all wearing steel plates we weren't born with," Erick said in a dark tone. "We all spent months, some of us longer, in hospitals. For the last two years we've done nothing but recover and work toward getting back to normal since it happened."

Jonas sighed and stood. He held out his hands for his weapons.

Badger handed them over without hesitation.

Jonas slipped them back into his holster and his boot. "I took a bullet, just missed my heart by a hair, and I was out for months. I can't imagine the damage done by a land mine. But vengeance, although it might have gotten you through the recovery process, is a pretty sick pill to be swallowing every day of your life. Answers are hard to come by with something like this."

"Which is why you can understand our trip here to gain even the smallest of leads to help get to the bottom of this."

"Now what?"

"Well, if you could find the shooter, we would much appreciate it," Kat said in a steely tone. "And then, given the fact that maybe the police have things calmed at my home and have picked up everyone responsible for the shootings and the murder of my uncle and God only knows what else, we'll be happy to go back to our normal lives."

"What is that normal life for you, Doc?"

"I'm a prosthetic designer. I work with all these men to try to give them full mobility again."

Jonas walked toward the door. "There's not a whole lot I can tell you. But, if I get any leads, I'll pass them on."

Erick handed him a card as he stepped out the door. "Stay in touch."

Jonas smiled. "I'd like to say it was nice meeting you, but ..."

Erick gave him a half grin and added, "Likewise."

CHAPTER 12

K AT SLOWLY LET out her breath. "How did he know you were here?"

"I came on my personal passport," Badger said quietly, and a lopsided grin slipped out. "I was hoping it wouldn't trigger an official investigation. The last time I was here, I might have had a problem."

She turned to stare at him. "*Might*? Enough that MI6 comes personally to see what you're doing?"

He shrugged. "I cleared it with them last time. I do have some connections in MI6. But Jonas isn't anyone I know personally." He glanced at Erick. "I guess the ranks have changed."

Erick nodded. "They always do. They always do."

Kat sank down on her bed and grabbed her laptop. "Well, that ate up a ton of time. We have to leave in the next half hour."

"So do what you need to do, and we'll leave."

The two men walked toward the door, engaged in conversation. She knew exactly what they were doing. And partly she was happy to let them. This was a tough-enough day already. She had no reason for MI6 to look into her. But just being associated with Badger apparently had been enough for them to find out all kinds of shit going on in her world. It just made the globe seem that much smaller too.

She checked her emails, sent off a couple to Jim, answered a few herself, and then found one from the detective. His phone number was on the email. She dialed it on the hotel landline and quickly called him. "Hey, it's Kat. Sorry for the late call. This time change is brutal. Do you have an update?"

"We haven't been able to find Paul's brother yet. He was released from jail two months ago, and he's not known at his listed address. By the way, you can return to your house while we tie up some loose ends. You'll obviously have to do some work and get the insurance moving."

"I called them," she said. "I'm waiting on a report. They should have been there yesterday."

"Good."

She heard papers rustling in the background.

"It's a case of stay low and let us work."

There wasn't a whole lot she could say to that. She ended the call, answered a few more emails, then realized it really was time to go. She shut down her laptop, put it in her bag, grabbed her sweater and walked to where the men were still discussing plans.

"It's time to go," she said abruptly. "I know there's all kind of shit still happening. I'm totally okay to go alone, but I need to go either way, right now."

The men stood glaring at her, then turned to look at each other, stepping back from the door. Erick opened it for her and said, "Get it in your head you won't be alone the entire time we're here."

"Good, that works for me. It means you get to drive because I wouldn't have a clue how to get where we're going." She grinned, smacked Badger on the shoulder lightly and added, "It also means you get to see the animals and look at

166

some of the new advanced technology they're using."

"Do you really think it'll work for humans?"

"Not widely today, not tomorrow. But it needs to happen soon. What we have in place works for many, but some need more."

They discussed some of the alterations that could be made as they drove to the vet's hospital.

At the hospital, the girl sitting behind the desk smiled and told Kat, Badger and Erick to wait in the reception area. Ten minutes later she was surprised to find Dr. Ron Macintosh standing in front of her. He held out his hand. "Delighted to see you. I've got an hour." He glanced at his watch and winced. "Not quite an hour."

"I appreciate you taking what time you do have."

There followed an hour that was as fascinating to her as it was to the men with her. Not only did they discuss what Dr. Macintosh was doing for various animals but he also showed her some of the prototypes they were working on, explained how the 3-D printing designs were sent away, and, when they came back, they actually did the implants. Then he took them for a tour in the back so they could see a couple of the latest animals he had worked on.

By the time she stepped outside the vet clinic, she wished she could have worked at his side for a couple weeks. She lifted her head and took a deep breath of the fresh country air. The men beside her stood quietly. She understood the feeling. What they'd just seen was both awe-inspiring and comforting.

"Do you think anybody is doing work like that in the US?"

"I don't know exactly, but certainly several vets are looking at it."

Badger looked at Erick. "Do we know any?"

Erick frowned. "Maybe Louise? Levi does security for her clinic. They had a big shoot-out there a couple months back. She's got a high-end HVAC system because of the bone-dust problems associated with her future prosthetics work."

"Amazing. Absolutely amazing."

As they walked back to the car, Kat felt a sense of wonder and potential soar through her. She knew transferring cutting-edge technology for the animals over to humans was a long way away. But there was just so much hope. Dr. Macintosh had achieved so much for those animals that it really made her heart smile.

As they reached the vehicle, Badger's phone rang. She came back to reality with a hard bump and turned to look at him. And waited.

"Talon, what did you find out?"

"Just like the MI6 guy said, nothing is here. However, I did track down a neighbor. He saw some man go into the apartment. He thought it was unusual because nobody had been living here. He was also carrying a large black case."

Badger's gaze flew toward Erick. "Did you get a description?"

Talon's voice filled the air so clearly she could hear too.

"He did get a glimpse. But not enough to ID him. He had on a black hoodie and a winter cap. He only saw him from the back. But we'll estimate six-two and lean. Didn't fill out the jeans and walked with a lanky kind of long loose step."

"Long arms?"

"Presumably. Goes along with long legs," Talon said in a dry tone.

Kat had to laugh because, of course, he was right. Most people were proportional.

The two men talked again for a few moments, then Badger said, "We're on our way back into London. I'm not sure there's any point in staying any longer."

"Have you heard from Mason?"

"No, not yet."

"Good enough. We'll meet you at the hotel."

Badger put away his phone, hopped into the driver's seat and said, "I'll drive."

Erick shrugged and got in the back seat.

With Badger driving, Kat got into the front. "This works for me."

He gave her a smile, reached over, squeezed her fingers and turned on the engine.

The drive back was pleasant. She studied the surroundings, realizing the sky was clear, and it might be sunny all day. "Can we play tourist today?"

"Sure. Is there any particular place you want to go?"

She shook her head. "I don't know the usual tourist places."

That started the discussion all the way back to the hotel about the merits of each tourist attraction.

Erick said, "We definitely have to go to a few places. We're booked to fly home on Monday. Today is Saturday. We might as well stay the extra day and a half. If nothing else, it will help us return to some normality in our lives."

Privately she agreed. "I want to see Big Ben," she announced. "And the wax museum."

"It'll be a long day tomorrow then," Badger announced. "You better hope the world lets us have the day."

She turned to stare at him. "Do you think we're in danger playing tourist for a day?"

He shrugged. "I wasn't expecting MI6 to spot us. So, outside of a shooter killing my informant, it's hard to say if we're in danger."

"We have to assume he saw you," Erick said. "You can try to minimize the danger all you want, but here's a thought. If he shot one person and left you alive, it was for a reason."

"Yeah, lack of opportunity," Badger snapped.

Back at the hotel they parked in the underground lot and made their way up to their rooms. Kat collapsed on the bed. "You know? I might just need a nap."

"I was going to suggest that. I have some work to do. The guys are all back at their rooms. We'll arrange to have lunch in, ... let's say, half an hour or forty-five minutes."

She thought about it. "That'll be good." So saying, she rolled over, pulled a blanket over her shoulders and fell asleep.

BADGER WATCHED HOW quickly she went out. He smiled. Like a child full of innocence, when the call for sleep sounded, she responded.

He pulled up his laptop, sat down and fired off an email to Mason. He knew it was too much to hope there might be news, but, at the same time, how much work could anybody do on an audio file?

Just as he sent off the email, he got one in. They crossed their communication lines. He read it and reached for his phone. Keeping his voice low, he said, "Mason, your email just came in. Are you sure about that information?"

Mason said, "Yes. Tesla went over it, and there's no way to do a voice recognition with the background noise, even when we took it off. But it definitely sounds like other voices. And little bits of conversation."

"So he was possibly in a group of people when he made the call?"

Mason hesitated. "Tesla identified a truck engine in the background, leading us to believe the speaker was inside a vehicle."

"Well, that makes sense."

"How well do you know the men in all three vehicles?"

"In the other two vehicles, as well as you probably do," Badger said slowly. "The men in my truck, very well." His voice took on an edge. "Is there any way to separate out background voices?"

"That's the thing. One of the voices in the background sounds like yours."

Silence. Badger thought his heart would stop. He closed his eyes and leaned against the headboard, his mind racing at the implications. "You think?"

"Tesla identified your voice immediately. When I heard it for the first time, I did too."

"Any other voices identifiable?" he asked in a very controlled tone. He was trying hard to not slam the phone against the wall. This was too important. But the thought that any one of the men in his unit could have betrayed them made no sense.

"I recognized Geir's voice. I think Erick's too. Definitely other men are speaking. And you might be able to identify them a little more yourself. But the caller, his voice, it's almost as if he used a mechanical device to change his tone."

"How big would something like that have to be to

change his voice?"

"It could be installed on the phone itself. In fact, it could have been a typed text message sent as a voice message. So keep that in mind. You might not have heard the true voice making the call. We only have a copy of the audio file. We don't have the original, and if, as you're saying, it's been deleted, chances are it'll be impossible to trace."

"Right. That's a hell of a bombshell."

"I know. But, if this is the audio file, and you're sure of its source, and the voices we're hearing in the background are as we suspect, somebody from your own vehicle, one of the men in your own unit, sent that message."

"But that would be suicidal," he exclaimed. "That makes no sense. Seven of us were badly hurt. One dead."

"Any idea of the mental states of the men at the time?" Mason's voice hardened. "Not to mention their allegiances?"

A muscle worked hard in Badger's jaw as he contemplated the thought. "I would have sworn on my life they were all patriots. And, if you were here in front of me right now, you know how close I would be to ringing your neck for even implying such a thing?"

"I know," Mason said with a note of humor. "It's not very nice to have to bring it up either."

Badger winced. "You're right, and I'm sorry. I did ask you to look into this. I just hadn't expected it to come back around to my own men."

"Sometimes when you open Pandora's box," Mason said quietly, "the only thing you find is a bit of personal hell."

"There's nothing *small* about this," Badger said, hating that a tremor made his hand shake. "This is major. As in, this is so damn big ..."

"Sorry. I suggest you listen to it yourself. Put on a set of headphones, close your eyes and hear for yourself." And Mason hung up.

Badger put down the phone, brought up the audio file, and, using earbuds to not awake Kat sleeping beside him, he hit Play and settled back to listen.

CHAPTER 13

K AT WOKE UP with an odd foreboding whispering across her shoulders. She rolled over on her back to see Badger sitting with his knees up to his chest, his arms crossed over top, staring off into the distance. The stony look on his face, the locked jaw ... Something was wrong. Slowly she sat up. He made no move to look in her direction. She got up, wandered into the bathroom, used the facilities and washed her hands.

As she walked back out, she realized he hadn't moved. Knowing it wasn't terribly wise, but not sure what else to do, she sat down beside him on his bed and hooked her arm through his. After a few moments she spoke in a low tone, her hand gently stroking up and down his arm. "What happened?"

He dropped his head back and released a heavy sigh from deep in his chest. "The audio recording I received ..." He let his head roll toward her. "There's a strong possibility it came from inside the vehicle my team and I were riding in."

She stared at him, not comprehending for a long moment. "What?"

He repeated slowly, "The call was made from inside the vehicle I was riding in myself."

She stared at him in horror, slowly sitting up, twisting to

face him. She gripped his hands hard. "You're saying one of the men you were with betrayed you all?" She searched his eyes, looking for any truth to this craziness. "How is that possible? He would have been blown up in the vehicle as well."

"I know." His words so simple, his tone so clear, left no doubt he couldn't believe it himself.

She turned her gaze to stare out the window. "Any chance it was a miscommunication? Wasn't intended to happen that way?" she asked, groping futilely for an answer. "Otherwise it suggests one of the men was looking to get killed."

"Or thought he could get away. And is even now covering his tracks."

She turned her gaze toward the door. "Surely you don't suspect Erick, Cade or Talon?"

He shrugged.

She could feel the color drain away from her skin—a cold clamminess wrapping around her heart. She just couldn't imagine how he felt. She pulled his arms apart and slid into them.

Instantly his arms relaxed, and she cuddled against his chest. So much pain resided in his gaze. She didn't know how to help him. The only thing she could do was offer what little comfort she could give him. Or what little comfort he would accept. He closed his arms around her and just held her close.

She couldn't fathom the sense of betrayal. "Is there any chance it's a mistake?"

"I don't know," he said quietly. "I've been thinking about that nonstop since I listened to the recording. I called Mason, and Tesla had done some work to clean it up, and he sent it back to me. But not before Tesla and he had recognized my voice. And the engine of the truck driving in the background. Which means the caller wasn't me." He gave a half snort. "Obviously. But seven other men were in the truck. And you've met four of them."

"I have. On my desk are more files," she admitted. "One I've turned down."

He twisted his head so he could look at her. But he didn't question why she had turned whoever down.

Maybe that was a good thing. Since being at the vet's office this morning, she'd wondered if some that she had turned down previously could have been helped in a different way. But it certainly wasn't today's issue.

"If it's one of the six other men, then the outcome obviously wasn't what he had expected. I don't think anybody chooses to get blown up and spend weeks, months, if not years in pain overcoming the physical disabilities. So I have to assume somebody either wanted to die or expected it wouldn't be as bad as it was."

The grip around her chest eased slightly as she contemplated that.

"And I highly doubt it was done as some kind of prank."

She shook her head. "No, of course not." She winced but knew she had to go forward. "What's the chance the man who died did it?"

His arms tightened around her again and then relaxed. "No. Mouse was the youngest of all of us. He was just a kid. Somebody we took under our wing and showed the ropes. He was fun-loving, bright, maybe too bright in a lot of ways. He was a good kid. He wasn't suicidal."

"Was he a joker? Was he somebody who would pull a prank like this?"

Badger shook his head. "Not like this. Definitely not like this."

"Of course he paid the ultimate price," she said for him.

He nodded. "That he did."

They sat together like that for a long moment. "Will you tell the others?"

His breath caught in his throat, and then finally he exhaled with a heavy breath. "I don't know what I'll do. I'd have sworn I could trust them all with my life. And have done so many times over, but now ... who do I tell?"

"Did you hear other voices? Did you recognize anyone's voice? Did you recognize the speaker's voice?"

"That's the problem. Whoever sent the message disguised his voice. It's computerized."

"How does that work?"

"You can get scramblers for calls," he said absentmindedly. "It comes out almost like a mechanical voice on the other end. This wasn't quite so techno. But it definitely made his voice impossible to distinguish."

"Meaning, he could have just had marbles in his mouth or something?"

That surprised a laugh out of him. "For the same effect, yes. It changed his voice, and I couldn't recognize it."

"Did you recognize anybody else's?"

He didn't say anything for a long moment, then nodded. "I think so. I think I've recognized three. The trouble is, seven of us are alive, and, out of all eight of us, seven of us have nothing to do with this. Seven of us are victims. There's just one asshole who decided to throw our lives up in the air and see where they landed."

"Surely you don't think it's one of your unit? You can't jump to conclusions."

"I know that. Before hearing that audio file, I would have said not one of them would have done anything like this. And that I trust them with my life. I have said so time and time again."

"Then stop worrying about it," she said gently. "You still have a lot of healing to do. If I had my way, I'd have you back in the hospital, having more surgery to fix that stump, so we can do better prosthetics. But you won't take the downtime in order to make that happen."

He sighed again, this time his hands gently stroking her back up and down. "You've got a good heart, Doc."

She chuckled and laid her head against his heart, hearing the steady pounding under her ear. "So do you. But you're bullheaded, stubborn and much too focused. And not on your own healing."

"It is on my own healing. But it's on a soul level. My spirit is damaged. My soul is hurting. And that audio file did not help."

She lifted her head slightly to stare at him. "And when you open Pandora's box, you have to expect what you'll find is not what you want to find."

He glared at her. "Mason said something similar."

She nodded. "So listen to both of us. Drop it. If you find any other information, then you can follow it. But, in the meantime, let's get you back to the hospital, get that leg fixed and get you moving on with your life."

"And what about the other men?" he asked in a harsh tone. "They deserve justice as much as I do."

She nodded. "They do. So pick the one you think you could trust the most and get him on board. And while you get your surgery, send him off and running to do what it is you need to have done. He can report back to you, and the two of you can figure this out."

"And the others?"

She shrugged. "Bring them in as you need to. And slowly knock off the ones who had nothing to do with this and find out the one who did."

He dropped his head back and stared up at the ceiling. "Easier said than done."

"Nothing about this is easy. But either you get your leg fixed, or it'll drop you."

"You drive a hard bargain."

She chuckled. "But you're not giving an inch, are you?"

His lips twitched. "I'll take it under consideration."

She knew that was as good as it would get. She twisted so she could look at his watch and tapped its face. "Isn't it lunchtime?" she complained. "I'm starving."

Just on cue came a knock on the door. She laughed, hopped up and ran to it. Opening it, before Badger had a chance to stop her, she froze. It wasn't Erick or Cade or Talon. But a tall lanky stranger, and the look in his eyes said he meant business. But the gun in his hand said so much more.

BADGER BOLTED TO his feet and slowly backed up, his gaze studying the man dressed in black. From the description he'd been given earlier, this man appeared to be the shooter who'd taken out his informant. Kat's back was stiff, and every step she took was like she walked on stilts. But she was doing as instructed. When she got close enough to Badger, he gently squeezed her shoulders reassuringly.

The gunman motioned at the two of them to move toward the bed. "Sit down."

Badger urged her backward with him. He had his phone in his back pocket. He entered the alarm code he and his unit had set up. It was a number only they knew. And it may help now. He managed to punch in the final digit, using Kat for cover. He wrapped her in his arms and gently tugged her to the bed, and the two of them sat down.

"Who are you, and what do you want?" Badger deliberately kept his voice low, calm.

The man gave a high-pitched laugh. "Well, I'll take the USB key you were given. And the money you were supposed to pay him."

"If you want either of those things, why did you shoot him?"

The man stiffened. "You don't know nothing."

"You killed the man and got nothing. How does that make any sense?" Kat snapped.

Badger admired her spirit, but he urged her to stay calm and to not set off the gunman's temper. It was hard to see the man's facial expression with the mask on, but the look in his eyes turned icy.

"You don't know anything." He waved the gun toward Badger. "Give me the money and the key, or I shoot her."

With the quick squeeze of her shoulder he popped the USB key out of the laptop and threw it at the gunman.

He easily caught it midair. "And now I want the money."

Badger got up, walked in front of Kat to his backpack, pulled it up from the floor onto the bed.

"Easy."

Badger slowed his movements, but he had to open the backpack to pull out the money. He reached inside, his other hand up as the gunman held his gun pointed on Kat. Badger did have a gun in his backpack, but the chance of getting it out and getting the shot off and not getting Kat hurt was minimal. On the other hand …

Crack.

The gunman swore and fell against the door, his gun dangling harmlessly from his fingers. Badger pulled out the gun he'd used to shoot through the backpack and held it on the gunman. He walked over, kicked his gun away, plucked the key out of his hand and tossed it to Kat. Then he pulled out his phone. He could hear racing footsteps outside the door. He quickly called Talon and said, "Come in, but a man's leaning against the door. I've shot him once. He won't make it."

His tone was dispassionate, cold. He quickly unlocked and opened the door enough that Talon could slide in. "We'll have to call Jonas of MI6. He's got a job we need him to do."

"Holy shit. What the hell's going on here?"

Kat came up behind Badger and crouched down beside the injured man. She placed fingers against his carotid artery and then shook her head. "You're a little too accurate with that thing," she said quietly. She stood and stepped back toward Badger. "How the hell did you get that here?"

"Talon brought it." He looped an arm around her shoulder and tucked her closer to him. "The shooter wouldn't have left us alive."

He knew her head turned to look at him, but he didn't want to take his eyes away from the man on the floor. The injured man made an ever-so-slight cough and collapsed the rest of the way to the ground. He gasped once or twice and stopped. That was called the *death rattle.*

Badger holstered his weapon, pulled out his phone, and, with the card Talon handed over, Badger quickly called Jonas. When the man answered, he brought him up to speed. "He's bleeding all over the hotel floor right now. But he's your shooter from last night."

"I'm on my way." Jonas hung up the phone.

Badger turned and led Kat back to the bed. "He's coming. Just sit down here and relax."

She shot him a look but behind it was temper. "I'm not being hysterical. I don't need to relax. But I sure as hell wouldn't mind going home."

"I have to admit I'm with you there." He turned toward the others and felt his leg give way as the metal pressed against the swollen part of his stump. He shuddered in place for a long moment, waiting for the waves of pain to ease back again.

Kat grabbed his fingers, just letting him know she understood. "You have to get that surgery."

He dropped her hand and forced himself to walk forward to join the other men. He might have to get the surgery, but he still had to get stateside in order to do that. Things had to happen in a certain way, and right now they needed to get rid of a dead man.

Talon handed him the man's wallet. Badger went through it, took a picture of the guy's driver's license and credit cards, checked to make sure nothing more was of interest and then handed it back.

Talon straightened. "Nothing else is on him."

"Well, he was hired by someone," Badger said in a harsh voice. "And he got one of his jobs done. Question is, was shooting us his second job or was he just cleaning up his first job? Or figured to collect a bonus for himself? But he knew about the money and the USB key."

"That implies he knows for sure you were in that hotel room when he shot the informant. It also implies he knew a deal was going down and the details."

"I already thought of that. Which just means my contact has either been hacked or our informant told someone."

They pulled off the man's hood and studied his face. They all took a picture of his face for ID. Badger quickly sent the shooter's photo to Mason, then to Levi. "I'm hoping someone can do a full workup on this guy."

As soon as word got out, all their phones started flashing. They looked at each other and grimaced. "Stone says he'll work on it," Talon said. He laughed. "Did all you guys contact him?"

"I contacted Levi. He's the boss."

Talon nodded. "Tesla's on it as well."

"Apparently nobody likes us getting shot at in England."

"I don't mind you getting shot at. It's when you guys shoot back, that's the problem."

At the strange voice at the door, they all turned.

Jonas stepped into the room, stared down at the dead man and sighed. "We've got paramedics coming. They'll take him away. But cancel the calls to the others. I think I know him. Low level hire. Been suspected of taking out a few high profile businessmen a couple of years back." He turned to look at the others. "And what makes you think this is the guy who shot your informant last night?"

Badger filled him in on the little bit they knew.

Jonas nodded and said, "If his gun matches, then fine. It's an open-and-shut case. I'll presume he either saw you in the informant's apartment building or saw you leaving." He stared for another long moment into each of their faces, then added, "When are you leaving town?"

"Monday."

He shook his head. "Your flights will be changed for free. But I'd like you out tomorrow."

The men nodded. "We can do that."

Jonas turned to look at Kat. "Sorry. Your visit is cut short. But your friends here bring trouble wherever they go."

She winced. "That's all right. I was just saying I wouldn't mind going home myself."

"Is it safe yet?"

Her face fell. Badger realized she hadn't considered the problems she'd be going home to. "Probably not, but I can get a hotel while my house is fixed." She raked her hands through her hair. "The sooner, the better. England's not looking like such a nice place to visit anymore."

CHAPTER 14

I N FACT, IT wasn't that easy to reschedule their flights. And it was well over sixteen hours later that they arrived back in the US. The decision was made that Kat would stay with Badger until they could figure out if her house would be fixed quickly or not. It was late; everyone was tired. Badger drove past her home so they could take a quick look, but, when she saw the busted window and the mess in the yard still to clean up from the glass, she shook her head and sat back again. There was only silence in the car as he drove to his house.

As they got out, she said brightly, "It's not exactly how I expected to come back to your house, but I will enjoy being here for the night."

He laughed. "That's the only reason you're my friend, isn't it? Just so you can stay at my place."

She tossed him a teasing glance. "Not necessarily. You're pretty good as a bodyguard too."

He shook his head. "Not so sure about that. England was not what I expected."

"That goes double for me," she admitted. "I had hoped for a little bit of tourist time, some relaxation from all the stress of what I'd been through. Instead, things geared up in a totally different way, and none of it was very good."

Badger led her inside his house and took her to the guest

room. She walked to the floor-to-ceiling windows on the opposite side of the room. She exclaimed in joy, "I don't know why you'd ever want to leave when you have this place."

"I wasn't planning on leaving for long. Home feels like my world is coming back to normal again."

She turned to watch as he dropped her bag on the bed, catching the pain that whispered across his face. She dropped her gaze to the floor and waited until he was done. It didn't seem to do any good to tell him anything. He needed to have the surgery that would reconnect more of the muscles to give him something for her to use as a base for a prosthetic.

But he wasn't ready for that step, and there was nothing she could do to force him to be ready. But still, he needed to get back on the crutches and let that stump heal.

He didn't say a word as he turned and walked out. She sighed, walked over to her luggage and opened it up.

He called back, "The pool might be a little cool, but it would be refreshing."

She headed to the window and stared down at the pool. The evening lights made the place look magical. "I'm game if you are," she called out.

"I'm already getting changed."

She laughed, found her bathing suit, walked into the bathroom, absolutely stunned at the gorgeous sunken bathtub, walk-in shower, double vanities. Everything appeared to be done in tile. Between the bronze and the gold and the brown with cream running through the tile, the colors gave it an opulent look.

She quickly changed, used the bathroom, washed her face and brushed her hair back into a quick braid, then grabbed a towel. In the suitcase, she found her beach cover-up, which she quickly threw over her suit. She didn't even know why she brought it, except if there had been a pool at the hotel, she didn't like walking up and down hallways or taking elevators in just her bikini. She'd always been very personal about her body, never an exhibitionist.

She walked down the stairs, seeing Badger at the bottom, waiting for her. Only there was one big difference. He didn't have his prosthetic on. He did have on shorts, and he was using his crutches. And a beautiful coonhound sat beside him, her tail doing a lovely sweep of the floor. Kat crouched down beside the dog and gently stroked her graying head.

"This is Dotty," Badger said by way of introduction.

The dog, hearing her name, jumped to her feet and barked. Kat laughed. "She looks happy to be home."

"And to go into the pool," he said, shifting his crutches away from the stairs.

She stopped, looked at the stairs and shook her head. "I never thought about how hard those stairs would be with the crutches."

He kept going, Dotty running between the kitchen door and the slow humans. "I'm used to it."

"I'm sure you are. Did you ever think about putting in an elevator?"

"I have the designs worked up and a price quote. But it'll be close to thirty thousand dollars, so I haven't gotten there yet."

"Ouch."

He laughed. "Yeah, ouch."

She followed him as he led the way through the kitchen and dining room area out to the back. Large full-size glass doors opened as he stepped to the right.

"Automatic doors?"

He nodded. "One of the last changes my father made after my accident."

She stopped and looked at him. "You lost him that recently?"

He gave her a grim smile. "They passed away six months after my accident."

"I'm so sorry. That was a double whammy."

"It was a rough patch." He walked over with his crutches to the hand rail, laid them on the side, pulled his T-shirt up over his chest, tossed it down and literally just fell into the water.

Dotty barked crazily and jumped in after him, swimming like a duck around Badger.

Kat laughed, quickly discarded her cover-up and unclipped her ivory leg. Tossing the towel on one of the chairs close to the pool, she dove into the deep end. The cool refreshing water broke over her body. She loved it. She rolled and twisted underneath the water until she needed to come up for air. When she broke through the surface, she was laughing. "Oh my. This is absolutely wonderful."

He swam toward her, a grin on his face. "So glad you appreciate it. I was wondering if I would have to come to the rescue. I didn't realize you were half mermaid."

"Growing up, I always thought that was the ideal person to be. I was in love with the cartoon *Ariel* and her underwater life." She smiled and brushed her wet hair off her face. "But to think that you get to come home to this every day ... You are very blessed."

"I am, and I know it. But it's not thanks to my own hard work. It's thanks to my parents."

"It doesn't matter how you got it. They created this heaven out of love. And they left it to you for the same reason. Obviously you'd rather they were still here with you, but, considering that can't happen, how lovely you get to have the memory of every bit of work that went into creating this place."

He gave her a smile that hit her deep inside. "Not many people understand that. Not many people know how I see the hammer strokes and the loving care. But, every time I look at a wall, I can see my father's hand placing the hardwood and the panels and the two-by-fours and his screwdrivers and drills in action. When I study the hardwood floors, I remember seeing my father on his hands and knees, checking the nails, checking for joints that weren't as good as they could be. And even more stripping and putting layers and layers of hard coating on top to protect them. My mother was always in the background, making him tea, shopping for materials for his next project and making sure he was looked after. They were quite the pair."

He gave her a lopsided grin. "My navy service gave me a view of the world, but my parents gave me a view of the opposite world. I don't know that I'd be the same person if I hadn't grown up knowing such a love was possible. Once I hit the service and traveled, I saw the crazy nasty things that people did to each other. It changed me. But still, on the inside, my parents' love inhabited that core that was always there with me."

She swam toward him, both of them just floating in the deep end, the colored lights magical outside. The evening was a little cool, but there was still some heat from the afternoon. It was just so damn refreshing and beautiful, she couldn't get enough. She flipped onto her back and floated.

"What your parents gave you was so much more than wood and money in this estate," she said quietly. "They gave you that loving foundation. And that's something you'll never lose."

They swam for several moments.

She floated, rolled over, dove to the bottom, came up and floated some more. She didn't ever want to leave. "With the lights around here, it's absolutely amazing."

"The lights give it a special touch." He paddled toward her. "We haven't eaten."

She rolled onto her stomach and looked up at him. "True, and I am getting hungry," she admitted. "But it's not like you have any food to cook, do you?"

He shook his head. "We could order in, or we could make something simple. I do have a little bit. Eggs and a few veggies. Maybe enough for a night or two."

She considered it for a long moment. "Honestly I'm hungry, so why don't we check out your fridge, if you're okay with that, and see what we can come up with?" Then she thought about it. "The trouble is, I don't want to get out. And I definitely don't want to get changed."

He laughed. "I have a special carpet in the kitchen, so we can go from the pool to the kitchen, make our food and come back out again."

"We don't have to get changed?"

He shook his head. "No, you can dry off a little bit, so we're not bringing in buckets of water, then come back out again."

"Done." She swam over to the ladder and climbed up to her towel and gave him space to get in and out on his own. Just like he'd become adept at crutches on the stairs, she knew he was adept at the pool but didn't want to make him feel any more self-conscious.

With her cover-up back on to keep the chill away from

the evening air, her leg back in place, she wrung the worst of the water out of her hair.

Dotty stretched out on the cement on the side of the pool and slept.

Badger wrung out the water from his shorts. When he was done, he grabbed his crutches, smiled at her and said, "Ready?"

Together they made their way back into the kitchen. He opened the large fridge and the two of them stared at the contents. "There's some leftover ham. We've got eggs and cheese, green onions, mushrooms ..."

"Perfect. You also have lettuce. You're okay if I make a salad?"

"As long as you make enough for two. And I'll fix a large omelet for both of us, if that sounds good to you."

Roles assigned, they went to work. It took fifteen minutes until they both held plates with the salad and half an omelet completely stuffed with mushrooms and ham. She smiled down at the dinner in front of her. "This is a veritable feast. Half the time I go home and grab an apple, and that's it."

He gave her a look of horror. "You need to feed yourself properly. Stress will wipe you out if you don't."

She nodded. "True enough but often I'm just so tired, and I have so much work to do, that I grab something fast and sit down and keep working."

"Got to stop that, Doc."

She grabbed the cutlery and both plates and headed outside. There was a small poolside table where she stopped, then her eyes took in the two lounges. "Do you want to sit in the lounges or at the table?"

He was already making his way to the lounges. Dotty,

caught by the smell of food, came over and lay down between the two loungers. Badger took one, put the crutches on either side and held out his hand. She passed him his plate and cutlery, then sat down on the one beside him. They dug in.

At her first bite, her mouth exploded with flavor. She sat back and relaxed. "You know? As a break, I could have just come here. Screw England. That was more stressful than anything."

He laughed. "If I had realized it would be so easy to look after you, I might have made that suggestion," he admitted. "But I figured you might have taken it the wrong way."

She turned her head so she could look at him. "The wrong way?"

He grinned. "Like I was making a move on you."

She leaned forward with a look of mock disappointment. "You mean, you aren't?"

He froze at the twinkle in her gaze and started to laugh.

She settled back and continued to eat, a satisfied smile on her face.

HE LOVED SEEING this side of her. The teasing, the laughter, and, for once, she appeared to be totally relaxed. She was correct. England had been a nightmare. As for dropping her stress levels and getting her to relax, it had done just the opposite. But here, at his place, she seemed completely chill. She was eating her food like she hadn't had a decent meal in forever. She'd taken to the pool like the mermaid she was.

He had to admit, the more he learned about her, the more he appreciated who she was on the inside. And he really loved the way they connected. He knew it was dangerous for him to think in that direction. He didn't want to be sidetracked from his goal. But, for the first time, he wondered if maybe he wasn't the only one who had to go after that goal.

He stared down at his stump. It was much happier after being in the water, but he knew by rights he needed to spend a full week on the crutches. And he should go back to the surgeon who had urged him six months ago to get the surgery. He was just putting off the inevitable, possibly to the point of not being able to fix the problem anymore. As Kat had said, she could do only so much. She had to work with what he presented her for flesh and tissue and bone structure. The surgeon wanted to go in and make it better, and Badger should be letting him. But that would mean walking away from this mission in his mind, the reason he'd gone to England.

"What are you thinking?"

He glanced at her, startled to realize he sat here with his bite of salad on his fork in midair. "Wondering about the surgery for my leg." He watched as her gaze went to the stump, and she frowned.

"You know as well as I do that the sooner you get it done, the better."

He nodded. "And how do I do that after what broke open in England?"

"Did anything break open? Or did it just lead you a little further down the path? And is this just for you to do? What about all the rest of the men who also experienced the same nightmare?"

He frowned, popped the salad in his mouth and chewed as he thought about her words. "I can't speak for the others.

I just know that it's been a driving force for me."

"But they appear to be at better stages physically. At least Erick and Talon. I'm not sure either of them needs surgery. You, on the other hand, need to take six months out of your life and get your own body a little bit farther along."

He nodded. "But I don't want to let go of my mission."

"Maybe it should be an 'our mission.' Not just yours. You got the information out of England. Maybe let it rest now. So you can move on, get your surgery done, while somebody else picks up the next leg of this."

He settled back, placing his empty plate on the side table. "I was just contemplating my options." He could feel her surprise. He smiled. "I know. I've been pretty focused on just doing the one thing."

"What changed?"

He frowned, clasped his hands together and dropped them over his belly as he stared up at the darkening sky. "It's hard to say," he hedged.

"No. For you to have made such a major shift, something has had to change. What is it?"

"Why are you asking?"

She frowned at him. "Because I care."

He studied her, saw the flush on her cheeks, the emotion in her eyes, and realized she really did care. But the big problem was, in what way? He had to know. He took a deep breath. "In what way do you care?"

Her eyebrows lifted, and her eyes dilated in surprise. She frowned. "What do you mean?"

"As a doctor or as a woman?"

The blush on her cheeks deepened, but she didn't look away. She didn't shift uncomfortably. Instead she stared at him with the same boldness he'd come to recognize from her.

"Both," she said quietly. "I certainly recognize there's something between us. I would love to see it develop." Her lips twitched. "Not just because I love your house."

At that he laughed. He reached for her hand. Without hesitation she placed hers in it. "In that case, I'll tell you the reason why my focus is shifting and why I'm rethinking my path of vengeance. Not that I'm letting it go but maybe broadening it to allow the rest of the men to take part—if they want to. I don't want to place this burden on their shoulders if they're content to walk away. Also they need to know about the audio file and make their own decision afterward. I can't keep this from them. I won't. There has to be an answer that doesn't involve one of us being the traitor."

She smiled and nodded, then pushed further. "And?"

"It's you," he said simply. "When I first met you, I didn't give a damn. I would go after this guy, and I would take him out. If I went out at the same time, I didn't care."

She nodded. "I could see that. It always bothered me."

"And you were never short on telling me that," he said in a dry tone.

She flashed a smile at him. "Somebody had to. You're too good a man to go on a suicide mission."

"Part of the reason why I didn't give a damn was because I had nothing here to hold me back. To make me want to come home again."

She studied him for a long moment. "You loved your family a lot, didn't you?"

"We were very close. My dad and I, we did everything together. And Mom, ... well, she was just very special. And, although I had a lot of relationships over the years, I never

found that special one. ... However, when I went on a
mission, I knew I had to come home for my parents' sake. It
would kill them if I didn't make it back. It almost killed
them when I was blown to shit. But they were here, right at
my side, helping me every step of the way. When I lost them,
I lost something else. I lost that root, that connection inside.
I lost anybody here who cared if I went or not—except
Dotty."

Dotty jumped up onto the lounger beside his good leg.
He stroked her back in long soothing strokes. "Dotty is great
company."

Kat shook her head. "It was hard on both of you. But,"
she said gently, "you still had your friends. You still had the
other teammates."

He nodded. "I did, but I could justify doing that to
them because I would be doing it *for* them too. I would give
them closure."

"Did you ever ask them if they needed it?"

He shook his head. "No. I don't even know if they all
know what I'm doing. Obviously Erick, Cade and Talon do,
but I'm not sure about the other three."

"Maybe you need to meet with them. Get it all out in
the open. Assign some duties. If you're on a mission,
everybody would have a part of the job. Everybody would be
tasked with something to do to help move this forward. To
complete the mission. You don't have to be a lone ranger. I
realize you were the team leader, carrying the burden of
responsibility and guilt for your team being blown up, for
losing Mouse. Yet you don't have to do this by yourself. You
never did."

He squeezed her fingers gently, sliding the thick pad of
his thumb across the long finger bones of her hand. "But I

felt alone. And, when you feel alone, you think you are alone. I saw this as my job. Something I had to complete alone. And that's what I've been grappling with this last year and a half. And I hadn't realized I wasn't alone any longer—had never been alone—until I went to England. With Cade and Talon and Erick."

She sat quietly, waiting.

He knew he had to get it all out to finish this. "In England, somehow I realized you were there. You were always there. Every time I turned around, you were there. Before England, some days—when I didn't have appointments with you—there'd be an email from you, telling me about results or a new plan. A new adaptation on my prosthetic or a new idea. I hadn't realized how much I loved opening up my email, hoping there would be something from you. How much I looked forward to our appointments. Even if only because I got to see you. When you were kidnapped, that was my first clue, my first scare. But I never really made sense of it all until in England, when the gunman held his weapon on you, and I realized just how close I was to losing you."

She smiled. "You know? It's funny. When that gunman arrived at our room, I wasn't worried."

"How could you not be worried? It's not like you've spent a lifetime at the other end of a gun."

She laughed. "No, but I knew you were there. I knew the others were there too. And I knew you wouldn't let him hurt me. It just wasn't your style."

He laughed. He gently squeezed her fingers once again. "No, but, for a moment there, I wasn't so sure. If he'd pulled that trigger, you'd be gone. And I knew then nothing would stop me from getting to the bottom of this. Even now I won't stop. You need to understand that. This is not something I can just turn away from. With this break in the case, I do want to bring in the other men. I'm hoping they can take the next step with my help and maybe allow me to get the surgery done. One of the other things that came to mind was the fact that, although I could do what I needed to do in England, if things had gotten much more physical, I don't know that my leg could have handled it."

"That's why you were wincing in the hotel room, isn't it?"

"Yes."

"Did something happen when you met the informant? Did you fall? Did you get injured?" She's swung her legs over on the lounger to face him, a frown forming on her face. "Did you hurt yourself?"

He shrugged. "It wasn't even so much that. It's just the leg gave out from under me because, of course, it doesn't fit properly. And I went down to try and help him, but it was already too late. And, by the time I searched the rest of the apartment and made it back to the pub, the leg was in much-less-than-prime condition."

She nodded. "And, if you hadn't had that happen then, you wouldn't have been reminded about the weakness of your leg. So maybe England was a good thing after all."

"England was a great thing," he said with a smile. "It helped a lot. I don't think it did you any good …" His eyes searched hers, looking for any signs of trauma from the last few days.

She shook her head. "It helped me too. No, it didn't give me the peace and quiet of a holiday. But it let me see the three of you in action. Four of you actually, once Talon arrived. It gave me a better idea of how you need to use your legs and what you are up against on a day-to-day basis when you're in the service. And it also let me see a different side of you. You never once tried to hide your disabilities. Even now I can see the scar tissue, the damage your body sustained ..."

"You've already seen it all, Doc," he said quietly. "No point in making myself look pretty. I'm well past that."

"But before, you were very damaged on the inside. Now I can see you're healing. And that's a very important step."

"I might never heal properly," he warned. "I still need answers."

"And you need to come to terms with the fact you might not get all the answers you want. And, in spite of it all, you have to put one leg in front of the other."

He laughed and lifted his stump slightly. "That would be a whole lot easier to do if it wasn't constantly soring up. The surgeon did say it wasn't a major operation but ..."

"It's not. It's just, after all the surgeries you went through, any operation was too much until now."

He nodded slowly, rubbing the top of the muscle. "I hate the idea of therapy work again."

"Not much of it this time. But you're not afraid of the work. You're not afraid of the pain. As a matter of fact, you've been incredibly dedicated to get as far as you have already." She studied his chest muscles. "The amount of muscle you have regained, the strength you have rebuilt ..." She shook her head. "It's amazing."

"I'm not pretty to look at."

She turned to stare at him. "Since when did I do pretty?"

At that he laughed. Because she was right. Everybody who walked into her door was damaged in some way. "I didn't expect, when I walked into your office, to meet somebody I would care about like I'm starting to care about you."

She shook her head. "I didn't expect that either. And there's no *starting* to care. You might be afraid of it. You might not trust it. But you already care—whether you're ready to admit it or not."

He smiled and pulled her slowly, inexorably closer to him. "You're right," he whispered against her lips. "I care."

And he kissed her.

CHAPTER 15

K AT LOVED THE feel of his firm lips against her own. She was afraid of hurting him. His stump was already sore, and she was in an awkward position, crushed half in his arms up against the lounge and half on the tile floor. But she didn't want to move. This was just so special, actually making it to this point in the relationship. He'd come through such major awakenings.

She was so damn happy that he had decided to do the surgery. She understood his reticence with all the pain and the problems he'd had up until now. But there was a time to quit, and this wasn't it.

She pulled her head back slowly, staring at him, her hand stroking alongside his face. "Wow. I wasn't expecting that."

He chuckled. "Maybe not, Doc. But resisting the urge was well beyond me."

She leaned forward and kissed him gently. And then wrapped her arms around his neck and hugged him. Dotty, as if sensing what was coming, slid to the ground and moved to lie a few feet away. Badger pulled her into his lap, twisting her up so her legs were over the side. She frowned at him. "Will this hurt you?"

He shook his head. "No, your weight is on the good side."

She smiled. "All right then."

They sat in each other's arms for a long moment. "I'll have to give him a phone call in the morning," he said.

She nodded. "You could be weeks getting a surgery date."

"I'll be lucky if it's not months."

She laughed. "True enough." She sighed happily. "I really want to go back in the pool, but, at the same time, I don't want to move."

"Well, I'd offer to carry you …"

She laughed. "No, definitely not. Maybe when you get a new leg on that stump but not right now." She disengaged her arms, sat up gently, and tried to keep the weight off his bad leg. She hopped to her feet and then held out a hand. "Maybe I can help you get to the water."

He rolled his eyes at her, hopped up in one smooth movement until he stood on his one strong leg, and he looked at the distance between him and the edge of the pool and his crutches on the far side of the lounger, and then back at her.

She tilted an eyebrow. "It takes a strong man to accept help when it's needed."

"And it takes a strong woman to actually ask for help when she needs it," he reminded her with a big grin. But his hand closed over hers.

Using her support, he made several hops to the edge of the pool and dove in. She followed at a slower pace. He was right. She'd had a hard time accepting any help several days ago. How soon she'd made major steps forward too.

When he broke the surface, she still stood poolside, minus her ivory leg, contemplating her own personal changes. He called out, "What's the matter?"

She shook her head and jumped in. When she broke through the surface of the water to gasp for air, she said, "I think we must be good together. We're certainly both growing and changing."

"Oh, we're definitely good together," he said.

He grabbed her and pulled her toward him. He was standing upright, but the water was too deep here for her, so she couldn't stand on her tiptoes. He wrapped her leg around his waist and tucked her up close. This time when he lowered his head, there was no exploratory tentativeness to his touch. He held her face, fingers firmly on either side of her head, as he kissed her. Heat sparked between them to a point she thought the temperature of the pool must be rising degree by degree.

She wrapped her arms around him and held him close, feeling his response at the heart of her. She'd never made love in a pool, but she couldn't wait.

When he finally released her, she didn't want to let go. She clung to his neck and kissed him back, her own need clawing inside her. She stroked her fingers through his hair, tugging as she twisted and slid her silky body in the water against his. Skin against skin, they stood for a long moment. When she came up for air, she gasped. "Wow."

He laughed.

When he tossed something behind her, she twisted to look, realizing that somehow he'd managed to take her bikini top off, and she hadn't even noticed. She stared down at her plump breasts pressed against his bare chest and smiled. "There is something lovely about a man who's good in the water," she said with arched eyebrows.

"You've seen nothing yet," he murmured as he pulled her down for yet another kiss.

He stroked up her back and around her shoulders coming up to cup her breasts. The feel of his hands, hot and firm, so different from her own soft gentle skin. He was hard everywhere, just bones and planes and muscles, scar tissue, damaged body parts blended into healthy body parts. He was such a man of contrast. But there was no mistaking his intent or his passion.

She didn't even realize when her bottoms came off. Or when he lost his own. But, when she slid her hands down his back to explore his buttocks, she slid one hand around to the front of him, finding just smooth skin and no material.

He twisted slightly to let her hand find his erection, hot, full and so damn big it was hard for her to do anything but stop in stunned amazement. She knew his physical dimensions almost as well as she knew her own. It was part of the research she had to do, part of the work she had to do to fit him properly for prosthetics. But at no point had there been anything sexual in her research. Now though …

By the low light, she slowly explored his full length, stroking, caressing, teasing, and when she finally slid her thumb over the slit at the top, he moaned in joy.

Before she realized it, he gripped her by the hips and shifted his position so she was now straddling him fully. With him placed at the heart of her, he slowly lowered her onto him. She gasped and froze, her body arching backward in the water as the waves lapped around them.

"Are you okay?"

She nodded. But trying to speak and breathe appeared to be too much. She sighed in joy. "I'm more than fine."

Instead of him controlling the motion, she slowly slid all the way down his shaft until he was seated deep inside her. The two of them sighed and moaned as she was sealed against him. She leaned forward until her breasts were pushed up against his chest. And she kissed him, her fingers stroking through his hair, rich, thick, lovingly caressing the curls, pulling them back off his face. He wrapped his arms around her and held her tight, letting the joy of being together overwhelm them both.

Slowly he stroked her back, her hips, her thigh, exploring the soft flesh in his arms. She leaned back, dropped her arms around his neck and smiled. "Can't say I have ever tried it this way," she murmured.

"We'll make it work," he promised.

She let her head fall back, her face tilted to the evening sky and started to ride. She moaned, her breath catching in the back of her throat with each stroke and slide as her hips rose and fell, a sweet delicious torment building inside.

And finally he pinned her up against the pool wall. "Sorry, I can't wait." He took over control, slamming into her over and over again until she was whimpering, helplessly caught in the throes of passion. Her climax broke, her cries flying free through the silent night. And still he drove deeper and deeper and deeper, riding her through her own orgasm until his body stiffened, his fingers on her hips clenched tight, and he ground himself against her, a long guttural sound filling the air.

He sagged onto her, his arms coming around to protect her from the cement on her back. She knew there'd be scrapes, and she didn't care one bit. It was worth it. It was all worth it. She wrapped her arms around his neck, kissed his cheek and just cuddled him close. Togetherness like this was worth everything.

Against her ear he whispered, "Okay?"

She leaned forward, smiled up at the worry in his dark

gaze and nodded. "Never better."

He grinned, kissed her again and said, "Now this is something I could get used to."

"I was just thinking that." And she laughed. The sound free and easy. And she knew they'd taken a corner she hadn't dared hope for. But she was so damn happy. She wrapped her arms around his back and lay her head against his heart. "I'm really happy right now."

He wrapped his arms around her and crushed her against his chest. "You and me both."

BADGER WANTED TO pick her up and carry her to his room and make love to her over and over again. But the sad reality was, that wouldn't happen. Until he got his leg fixed and could wear a prosthetic properly, such debonair moves were beyond him. He knew it wouldn't matter to her, but he wasn't the man he wanted to be.

When he was whole and healthy, he could have carried her to his bed with no problem. Making love like this would show every unpleasant defect he could possibly have. That she'd already seen his records and most of his body didn't seem to make one bit of difference when it came to intimacy at this level.

He slowly separated from her. "Do you want to stay down here or go up to my room?"

"Let's go to your room," she said quietly. And, as if understanding his discomfort, she made her way out of the pool and grabbed the towel again. He watched as she slipped on the beautiful ivory leg. He'd seen her casualness, her acceptance of her physical state and knew he had a long way to go in that regard. But, with her here, to keep it real, he knew he'd get there. She dried off and collected the dishes. "I'll take these into the kitchen."

He made his way out of the pool, sat down on the side of the lounge and dried off. Then he grabbed his crutches, the towel she'd forgotten and his towel, and made his way inside. He leaned against the countertop and stared at her as she deliberately avoided looking at him. "Doesn't look quite the same in the light of day, does it?"

She turned to look at him in surprise. "What?"

He motioned to his leg and the crutches.

She stopped and stared at him for a long moment. "Do you think for one moment I give a damn?"

There was a steely hurt tone to her voice, and he realized he'd let his own insecurity be the filter by which he had judged her. He shook his head. *"It's not you. It's me."* And he gave her a lopsided grin.

She took several steps forward and glared up at him. "Don't. Don't make fun of this. I won't make fun of your wounds, your injuries, the pain you've been through. But neither do I intend to knock the man you have become because of it. This"—she waved at his new form—"is beautiful, with or without the second leg. And don't ever forget that."

She reached up and kissed him hard, adding, "And don't ever say that again."

CHAPTER 16

K AT WOKE IN the morning slowly, with a sense of well-being deep inside. As she opened her eyes, she found herself wrapped in Badger's arms. She wasn't a small woman by any means, but he was huge. With her head on his shoulder and her arm across his chest, he looked like a mountain of muscle beside her. She smiled, rolled her head toward him to see if he was awake. He was lying on his back, staring at the ceiling. Although he was resting, his gaze was open, and she could see the wheels of his mind turning.

"Did you have a good night?" she whispered.

He tightened his arm around her and cuddled her close. He leaned his head to the side and kissed her on the forehead. "The best."

She chuckled. "As much as I really enjoyed our nighttime activities, I was more concerned as to whether you got any rest."

His lips twitched in a lopsided grin. "I got enough."

She sat up and stretched, uncaring when the sheet fell to her waist. When his hand slid up her back and around to cup her breast, she leaned over him and smiled. "Surely you're not still in the mood."

He gave her an innocent look. "I'm male. That means I'm in the mood."

She burst out laughing, kissed him and said, "That may

be. But think of the pool as foreplay."

She sat up, clipped on her leg and went into the bath-room. When she was done, she stood and stared at the image in the mirror. She looked happy. She looked well loved, her hair tousled, a sleepy slow-eyed look to her eyes, and a rosy flush to her skin. In truth, she had never looked better.

She wandered back out to the bedroom to find Dotty lying on the bed where Kat had been lying. "She's quite the opportunist." She glanced around.

When he didn't answer, she turned to see him sitting on the edge of the bed, wrapping the cloth around his stump.

She stopped, put her hands on her hips and said, "Crutches not the prosthetic."

He glared at her. She pointed at the inflamed flesh. He looked back at his stump and nodded.

She walked closer, her fingers gentle as she examined the puffy skin. "Do you have any cream for this?"

He opened a night table drawer and pulled out an anti-biotic cream.

She brushed his hands away and gently coated the angry tissue. "Better if you wear shorts and pin it back to leave this open and free for the air."

"Only if we're staying home. If we're going anywhere, that's ugly as hell."

She frowned but kept her own counsel. She'd much ra-ther he did what was better for his body than worry about what it looked like. But she understood that not everybody appreciated seeing something like this. She straightened and stepped back. "Speaking of that, what are we doing today?"

"Well, apparently we'll start with a swim," he said, com-plaining.

She laughed and looked around. "I would ask where my

bathing suit is."

At that, he chuckled. "Probably where my shorts are," he said drily.

She winced. "There's nobody down there, right? Nobody would have seen that?"

"I live alone. I don't have a gardener who comes in unannounced. Although I do have somebody who comes once a week to clean the house. It's not her day today."

"Good. Shall we go down in our birthday suits and find our clothing?"

He nodded, grabbed his crutches and straightened up on his good leg. "Lead the way."

She snickered. "You just want a view as you walk."

"Damn right I do," he said cheerfully. "My mama didn't raise no fool."

She walked slowly and carefully, feeling an odd sense of freedom with the fact that she was completely nude. She'd wondered about grabbing something to cover up with, but it seemed a little odd to dress just to go downstairs so she could put her bathing suit back on. In fact, it would feel very strange to put a bathing suit back on when they'd been nude up until now.

Down in the kitchen, the big double doors opened, and she peered outside. Dotty raced into the morning light. No one else was there. Kat stepped out, loving the feel of the fresh air on her skin. She found one of her bathing suit pieces on the edge of the pool; the other lay on the bottom of the shallow end. She stood and stared at it. "There seems to be something logistically wrong about going into a pool nude in order to grab clothing so I can put it on." She turned toward him.

He had his shorts in his hand as if about to step into

them. He looked at her. "You don't have to get dressed for my sake."

She stared at him and realized she'd never in her life gone swimming in the nude. She unclipped her leg and with a big grin took several hops forward and jumped into the pool. She gasped at the cold water. She rolled and swam and frolicked. She put on her bathing suit bottoms, then retrieved her top. With that back on again, she said, "So weird to think this is a much more natural feel."

"Considering I think I hear a vehicle out front, it's probably a good idea too."

She stared at him in horror and glanced around the pool. "Five minutes ago, they would have gotten an eyeful."

"As far as I'm concerned, you're still an eyeful in that outfit. It doesn't hide much."

She glanced down at her long lean form and said, "In truth I don't have much to hide."

"But what you have is prime, so I'd rather the guys didn't get a look."

With her cheeks fire-engine red, she plunged back under the water and started to swim. She set herself up into a rhythmic motion of laps. Going from one end to the other until she could feel her muscles tire. She finished at the shallow end and turned her face out of the water as she just floated in place.

"Kat, the guys are here."

She looked up to see the men staring down at her. She smiled. "You could come in."

"We would have if we'd realized you would spend the morning lazing about," Erick said with a grin, crouching at the side of the pool, cuddling Dotty, who was ecstatic to see them.

"It was a good way to start the morning." She swam toward the steps, grabbing her towel from the railing. She didn't remember it being there before so presumed Badger had placed it along the metal pole.

"We'll meet you inside," Badger said, as the men followed him, Dotty tagging along at the rear.

He was giving her a graceful exit from the pool to put on her prosthetic. She hopped out, drying off a bit before attaching her prosthesis. Then she wrapped the towel around her and entered the house. "What plans have we got for the morning?"

"We figured we should run past your house first," Badger said quietly. "You probably want to check in just to see that everything's okay. Plus we can call to find out what the police have found, what we have to do to secure your property so you can move back in again."

She knew he was right, but the thought of leaving this wonderful idyllic paradise was a little more than she wanted to comment on right now. "Before we do all that, I need food."

She left the men talking while she walked into the kitchen. She vaguely remembered the contents of his fridge but didn't know if Badger needed something substantial or just a bite. She stood in front of the open door and wondered if she should make another omelet.

He called out, "Not sure how hungry you are, but there's yogurt, fresh fruit and granola, any of the above. If you find something you want, grab it."

She wandered over to the pantry, found the granola, headed back to the fridge, grabbed blueberries and yogurt and quickly made herself a decent-size bowl. She put on coffee while she was here, grabbed a spoon and headed outside where the men were gathered again. She sat down on the lounge she'd been on last night, and, with the towel still wrapped around her, she ate breakfast. Then she caught something about Erick leaving. "Where are you going?"

"I'm heading overseas, where we were injured. Tesla caught the sound of something else in the background. A repeating station was over there. She said she could hear it in the background."

Kat stared at him, slowly lowering her spoon to her bowl. "What good will that do?"

He shrugged. "I don't know. But I can't quite let go of the fact somebody did this. Especially after hearing the audio myself."

"I get that. But what will going back to the scene do? It's not like any evidence will still be there after all this time, would it?"

He shook his head. "No, probably not. And I hate to say this, but I have nightmares that just don't quit. I was thinking, if I went back, I might be able to put some of those to rest."

"And check with the locals to see if anyone knows anything helpful, I presume?"

"Not the locals," he said with a hard smile. "It'll be the rebels who planted that antitank land mine."

Badger started beside her. "I wonder if it was planted on purpose."

She turned to look at him. "Of course it was. It's not like that was an accidental land mine," she half joked.

He looked at her, and she could see the darkness inside.

"Are you thinking it was actually planted, buried for your vehicle? Not just that someone knew it was there and sent your vehicle in that direction? That's a whole different level of ugly."

His gaze shifted to the other men. "What do you guys think?"

There was tension in the air as everyone contemplated such a betrayal. Erick nodded. "It's very possible. I'll go have a little talk over there on my own."

"I'm coming with you then," Cade said. "I don't have anything happening anyway. I've got no job, no money to burn, and, like the rest of you, it's hard to move forward until this is settled."

The two men high-fived each other. They both turned to look at Badger. He nodded. "I think it's a great idea. We know a supplier too. He might have a lead on who bought the land mine. I think I should go too."

"No." Kat's voice was calm and sharp. "You need to get that leg fixed."

He'd tugged on his shorts, the length covering his stump. He glanced at her. "It can wait a few weeks."

She shook her head. "No. That flesh is inflamed, and it's not getting better. If you lose any more of your leg, I won't be able to put a prosthetic on it. You'll be left with much less than you have now. Everything we lose at this point will impact your mobility down the road."

He glared at her.

She glared back. "You know I'm right."

His fist clenched, and he opened his mouth to say something, but the words didn't come out.

She reached a gentle hand across and placed it on his hand. "No. Erick and Cade can take care of this part. You took care of London. Let them do this one. A few weeks, a few days even, will make a huge difference to your leg."

"They can delay this for a few days. And then I can go

with them," he growled.

She shook her head. "I think they want to go now." She turned to look at them.

Both men shrugged their shoulders and nodded. "Yeah, we kind of do." They looked at Badger. "I know you don't want to go back in a hospital, and I know you don't want to give your body the time it needs because you're done with all of that," Erick said, his tone understanding, yet implacable. "We're all in the same boat. Not one of us wants to sign up for more of what we've been through. Not one of us wants to lie in a hospital bed again. And you can bet not one of us wants to go through any more therapy. But the fact of the matter is, your rehab is not done. And you need to complete it. You found the first pieces of information and a lead. That lead has led to something else. Let somebody else step up and take care of the next part. We often went off one or two at a time when we were on missions because we had assigned jobs. Let this be Cade's and mine."

Badger gave a heavy sigh. "When are you planning on leaving?"

The two men glanced from Badger to Kat and then back again. "We'll go with you to Kat's house this morning and take a look. We'll try to leave this afternoon."

Badger stiffened.

She squeezed his fingers and said, "Accept it."

He sagged in place and nodded. "You call if you need any help. I don't give a shit if I'm in the hospital or not, you know I'll come."

The men nodded. "That we will. We're kind of hoping you might run the control center on this one. Stay here, be at the end of your phone at all times, get us information. You know what transmissions and communications are like over there. I don't want to put Mason or Levi in any position of having some of this come back on their shoulders. If we contact you, you can contact them."

Kat watched and listened as they worked out the details.

When Badger asked, "Do you need any funds to make this happen?" both men shook their heads.

"We're good. If we need bribe money, we'll call you."

Badger nodded. "Just make sure you go in with enough to get through the first part. Who's to say where this one will go? But, if you do find anything about that land mine ..." and he let his voice trail off.

Cade nodded. "That we can do." He walked into the kitchen and returned with coffee on a tray for everyone.

Kat realized these guys knew Badger's house better than she did. They had been here many times over the years. Proof of their friendship. Proof of a life she didn't know anything about. They were also very well loved by Dotty. Something she knew would develop over time with her if she were here long enough too.

As soon as they finished the coffee, she went upstairs and got changed. She wanted to go to her house and get that part of her life together. As much as she loved being here with Badger, she didn't want to push the relationship. She was already prodding him for that surgery and to take the proper time to heal. She was in a hard place as far as becoming his girlfriend. They were lovers, but, in this day and age, what did that mean? Back downstairs again, she collected her stuff, put her wet bathing suit in a plastic bag, and, when she was ready, set everything at the front door.

By this time Badger was dressed and coming out of the office. He was using his crutches, which was good for him, but she knew he was only doing it for her sake. When he saw the bag with a bathing suit, he shook his head. "You're not staying at your place tonight."

She frowned at him. "Why not?"

"You don't have a kitchen window for a start. And we don't know what we might have to do to get your security back online."

She glanced around and said, "I didn't want to be a burden here, to overstay my welcome."

"Enough of that talk. Put your bathing suit outside on the back of the lounge so it'll be dry when we return. You can hit the pool a second time then."

She was torn. But it didn't make any sense to leave her wet bathing suit in a plastic bag if she couldn't leave it at her house. Silently she followed his instructions.

When she met him at the front door again, all the men were gathered around. They drove two vehicles over to her house.

Pulling into her driveway, her gaze locked on the busted window, hating the desolated appearance the house had, the property, the neighborhood. When she glanced at Badger, his gaze was on everything but the house. He was still in protective mode—his eyes searching and missing nothing. She hopped out and waited until he joined her. With Erick and Cade beside them, they walked slowly through the property.

She brushed her hair back. "I need to phone the insurance assessor."

"And see if he was actually here," Badger said. "He might not have come if you weren't here."

"He was supposed to." She pulled her phone from her pocket and dialed the number. She walked through to the living room. When she got the assessor on the line, she got confirmation he had been here.

"We are clearing your claim," he said. "I suggest we get a restoration company, and they can do it all for you."

"Yes, I'd rather have that. They can handle all the rest of this headache and get it back to rights without me losing hours contacting contractors."

"Let's do that then."

With an appointment set for that afternoon with the restoration company, she wandered about, noting the flooring had been gouged by the shattered glass. The linoleum in the kitchen had several recent cuts in it as well. How very sad. Upstairs she stood in the doorway to her bedroom, crying out in shock.

From behind her Badger called out, "What's wrong?"

"Somebody has completely messed up my bedroom," she cried out. "In other words, people came in and took what they wanted while I wasn't here."

"Definitely a problem." He approached from behind her, took one look and said, "Whoa, this is more than somebody just messing up the place. What's the chance somebody was here looking for those coins?"

Her breath caught in the back of her throat. "It's very possible. But they sure as hell aren't here."

A voice from the spare room said, "Where the hell are they?"

She spun to see a man she'd never seen before holding a gun to her and Badger. Under her breath she whispered, "Shit."

The gunman nodded. "You can swear all you want. And it's nothing to what you'll be crying out if you don't start talking."

She held out her hands. "What are you talking about?"

"The big guy said it already. Where are the coins?"

She sucked in her breath. "I guess you're in cahoots with my lovely brother Teddy, are you?"

The man's eyebrows rose. "Teddy is a piece of shit."

"That he is," she said cheerfully. "But he's still my brother."

"That's okay. He'll spend a lot of years in jail."

She frowned. "And you won't?"

He shrugged. "It's Teddy's word against mine. That means nothing to the lawyers."

"You're Paul's brother, Jackson, aren't you?"

For the first time she saw a crack in the man's confidence. "What do you know about Paul?"

"I know you guys hired him to kidnap me, or shall I say, forced him to kidnap me, bring me here so you could get the coins. You're also the letter writer. Nice touch."

The gun waved in front of her. "That wasn't me. That was your brother Teddy."

"But you supplied information and your brother as a victim."

"I might have mentioned my brother's existence to Teddy, but that's it."

Her mind moving quickly, she sorted out how best way to get this guy to admit everything. Because, so far, he was right. It would all just point to her brother.

"Well, somebody is still paying you."

The man's face split in a grin. "Yeah, somebody is."

"That would be my aunt then."

Both his eyebrows shot up. "Your aunt's a good-looking woman."

"But then you're sleeping with her, so you would think that."

He frowned. "Enough of this shit. Where the hell are the coins?"

"Why didn't my aunt steal them in the first place? She didn't need you and Teddy involved in this."

"She couldn't find them. Stupid bitch. She had a lot of time where she could have moved things, tucked them away for later. But she never did."

That's about what Kat expected. Her aunt was a piece of work. "They're in a safe-deposit box at the bank," she announced. "Why the hell would I keep something so valuable here at the house?"

"Well then, guess we're going on a road trip." He motioned with the gun. "Turn around slowly and make your way down the stairs. No funny tricks. The big guy behind you is already suffering. Don't know how well he'll operate if I blow the knee out of his good leg."

She could feel Badger stiffen behind her. But she knew it wasn't because of the threat against him. It was more that this asshole would even attempt to threaten them. She nodded and said, "Okay, but don't go gun crazy here. My poor place has already been damaged enough."

"Yeah, I'll just torch it after this."

Angry, she made her way around Badger and slowly walked down the stairs. Erick and Cade had arrived and were entering the living room. They waved at her as she came around the landing. Badger stomped his way down behind her with his crutches. She knew the gunman wasn't far behind. She waved in a panic and motioned behind her. The two men stopped in confusion until Badger came into sight, and they saw his face.

Instantly they disappeared from view. She took the last step down. She wasn't sure if Badger would try and take the gunman out or wait for help from his friends. As she walked to the front door, she turned to see how Badger was doing.

He mouthed, *Keep going.*

"No talking. And no funny stuff. I didn't come all this way to lose now."

She shrugged, stepped through the front door and held it open for Badger. She couldn't imagine getting two people into a vehicle while holding a gun on them and expecting them to drive him to the bank. She understood the fear behind a gun, but somehow, over the last few days, she'd even lost a lot of that. She had a lot of respect for the damage the bullets did, but she had more respect for Badger.

The gunman had no idea what was coming. As Badger stepped out the door, she caught sight of Erick hiding behind the door. As the gunman exited, Badger pivoted, lifted his crutch, slammed it hard against the gunman, at the same time reached out, grabbed him by the wrist and pushed his hand into the sky. Reflexively the gunman fired several shots harmlessly into the air, but he was already falling to the ground as Badger came down hard on his good knee to his chest. The two men flipped and rolled as they fought.

She slid her knife out of her special ankle sheath and waited for the opportunity. She was damn fed up with being accosted. Especially in her own house. She caught the pain in Badger's face as he came down hard on his stump and flipped the intruder to his back ...

Jumping in, she held her knife to the stranger's throat and ordered, "Stop."

Both men, chests heaving, stared at her in shock.

But something in her gaze made them believe her. The attacker relaxed and groaned. "Fucking hell."

"Yeah, that's one way to say it," Erick said from behind

her. He gently motioned Kat out of the way. "Nice job, Doc." Erick gently removed the gun from the man's hand and turned it so it faced him.

Cade arrived to hold the intruder in place as Erick helped Badger to his feet. Kat knew better than to mother him, but, at the same time, the white tautness of his expression spoke volumes.

Cade turned to her. "Where'd the knife come from?"

She gave him a bland stare.

A wicked grin lit his face. "Come on, Doc. Give ..."

She lifted her pant leg to show the hidden sheath. While they watched, she tucked it back into place. They whistled in approval. She stepped back and tapped her heel against the sidewalk. Instantly a blade popped out the toe.

Fascinated, the men started talking all at once.

"Have you got a gun in there somewhere?"

"No, ... not on this leg."

The grins split their faces in two. "You'll design me one, right? Where I can keep a blade and a gun without anyone knowing?"

Cade jumped to the front with his request, but Erick wasn't far behind. He stared at her leg in fascination. "It completely blends into that scrollwork design. The leg is feminine, practical and extrafunctional. I love it," he declared. He turned to Badger. "I want one."

"A feminine leg?" Kat asked with a straight face.

The men chuckled. Badger, his color slowly returning, said, "You never told me about these designs."

She raised an eyebrow. "What was the point? You're not in the market for anything like this until you get the surgery."

Mixed emotions slid over his features.

Good. Let him stew about that for a bit. After she'd seen the pain he was in, she'd rather have him in bed for a full month to get the tissue to heal properly just to be able to have the surgery but wasn't sure there was time. If those veins collapsed …

Stepping back, she pulled the phone from her pocket again and called the detective. Once she brought him up to speed, she turned to the men. "The cops are on the way." She looked at Badger. "I don't know if we want to just leave him here, but I really don't want that piece of shit back in my house."

Erick pulled out a pair of handcuffs from his back pocket and secured the gunman, leaving him lying on the ground. "He's not going anywhere." He glanced around at the house. "You shouldn't stay here. It's not horrible, but you'll need a couple weeks to get it back to normal."

"I wonder if it'll ever be normal," she said, the shock settling in. "A lot's happened. I won't look at it the same way again."

Erick nodded. "You'll need time to get over all this. Once you get everything fixed, it'll look a lot better."

She wandered the front yard, looking at her house, waiting for the police to arrive. She was glad it was over. She doubted her aunt would cause much trouble. The fact of the matter was, the police had probably already picked her up. If not, they would soon. She didn't know what the end result would be, but the last thing she wanted was anybody to have another thought about coming back and killing her.

She walked over to the gunman. "What would you do with the coins?"

He stared at her. "Sell them of course."

"Yeah, that's what I think I'll do too. My uncle wanted

me to keep them, but it seems like he died for them, and there's been a lot of hell since."

"A lot of lives ruined over something like that," Badger said. "But if you want to keep them as a memento of your uncle …"

She shook her head. "I have my memories. I think I'd rather sell them and move on."

"They're worth a shit ton of money," the gunman roared. "That bitch said I could have half."

"Well, since that bitch killed my uncle, chances are we just saved your life," she snapped. "Because you were never going to get half."

The cops pulled up just then. By the time the gunman was led away, the detective was grinning like a madman. "Thanks for this guy. We just picked up your aunt too. Soon as she saw us coming, she knew she was in trouble. She's already confessed to killing your uncle."

Kat nodded. "Of course she did." She shook her head. "If everybody confesses, do I have to testify?"

"No, as there wouldn't be a trial in that case. We'll need a statement from you though," he said. "At least now you can relax and move forward with your life."

He pulled away with his prisoner, and she watched them disappear down the street.

BADGER WRAPPED AN arm around her shoulders. He tucked her up against his chest. "I'm glad to have that done."

She twisted to look at him, to kiss his cheek. "I am too. Just how very sad for my uncle."

"A lot of people got caught in that net. Greed will do

that."

Together they shifted to look at the front of her house. "It wouldn't be so bad—except for the flooring that has to be redone, then replacing two windows, the hot water heater and the circuit box."

"That's not your problem. The insurance will cover it."

She nodded. "But not for weeks."

"And that's why you'll be my guest for a few weeks." He wondered what it would take to make her a permanent guest. This was a nice little house, but it was nothing like his place. But, if she rented this, it would give her a nice nest egg in case she ever needed it. Not that he ever wanted to see her in that position. He had plans for her. Long-term plans. He could only hope she'd go along with them.

She twisted and slipped her arms around his chest and laid her head against his shoulder. "Are you sure you want a guest that long? Although we've known each other for a while, we haven't been together very long."

"Yes, we have," he said comfortably. "We know who each of us is on the inside."

She squeezed his torso hard and smiled. "I won't say no because I love your house."

"Hey, you're supposed to come for me, not for my house."

She tilted her head back, looking up at him. "In truth, I think I'm falling in love with you too," she admitted.

His heart stopped and then raced forward. He gave her a slow smile and whispered, "I would love that very much." His hand slid up to hold her head, his fingers stroking through her locks of hair. "For the longest time I didn't think life would be worth living. I was bent on getting my vengeance any way I could, and I didn't care if I survived or not. But that's all changed now. Because of you. I don't have to do this alone. I can let others help out, and taking care of myself has become a priority. I want a future now. I want a lifetime—with you." He leaned forward, holding her head steady and kissed her gently on the lips. "You saved my life too. And if you save a life …" He grinned a big fat smile and finished, "… then you're responsible for the rest of that life."

She chuckled and leaned back. "Does that mean you'll stay close to me so I can do that?" Her tone was warm, sexy.

His heart melted, and he crushed her against him. "Absolutely."

EPILOGUE

ERICK FULLER HEFTED his bag in his good arm and walked toward customs. Cade was only a few seconds behind him. They were traveling together but separate. They'd sat in different areas on the plane so nobody could tag them as being together. As soon as Erick cleared customs and headed out toward the front entrance, he took a moment to adjust to the heat. Being in Afghanistan brought back a lot of memories. It had been one of the reasons for the fast decision to come over here. The longer he stayed home and knew this trip was happening, the worse the nightmares would get. He hated to even let anybody know he was having them.

But his shrink knew. PTSD was a real issue. And nothing seemed to be working for him.

He was hoping answers would help. While he waited for Cade to join him, he texted Badger that they had landed safely. Confirmation came immediately. Badger would be at the end of his phone at all times, to run control in case they needed anything. This could be a twenty-four-hour trip, or it could be much longer. They were renting a rig and driving out to the area where the incident occurred, would talk with the local villagers and then come home. Okay, so maybe two or three days tops.

But he didn't expect it to be any longer than that. Longer would mean they either ran into big trouble or found a big lead. After two years he doubted there were big leads to find, and there was way too much trouble in this part of the world already. He'd like to avoid that if he could.

They were meeting up with an old connection. Somebody who would supply them with the weapons for the trip. He didn't want to take the chance of crossing borders and getting stopped. He could have, but it was risky. He traveled under his own passport too. He hadn't been flagged in England; that had been Badger who had popped up. But then he'd had a few issues, and MI6 always seemed to keep tabs on him. Erick chose to travel under his real name and see what came of it. If anybody asked, he'd tell him this was a nostalgia trip.

And that was the truth, in part.

The hot sun beat down on him. Then what the hell did he expect? There was just such a different smell to the air here. He preferred traveling through places like Canada and Siberia. There was a freshness to the coldness there. It brought its own chill but killed off any of the old heavy air that seemed to settle in hot places. And when the wind did come through the hotter climates to clean out the old air, it brought with it sand and dust that choked your throat and filled your lungs and made your nostrils snort futilely for weeks. He couldn't believe he was back here. It was so not where he wanted to be.

A hard hand landed on his shoulder. He turned to see Cade. He nodded. "Ready?"

"Almost. I know you said you wanted to run this with just the two of us. But, before leaving, I got a text from Talon."

Erick raised his eyebrows. "I guess we should have expected that after England."

Cade nodded. "He wants in."

"Not sure that's a good idea. You heard the audio file yourself."

"I know. But I can't believe Talon, or any of us, had anything to do with the incident."

"I'm with you there. I just wish the audio was clear enough to be sure it wasn't one of us who made the call that gave away our location."

"I hear you."

Just then a shout sounded from behind them, and Erick turned to see Talon walking toward him. "Wow, he's fast."

"He was already here. Well, close to here anyway. He got in a few hours ago. He's been waiting for us to land."

The men exchanged greetings. Talon smiled at Erick. "I hope this isn't a problem. I know Cade didn't get a chance to talk to you before he okayed it for me."

Erick shrugged. "We're always glad to have you around. We do need to get answers. It just sucks the audio file appeared to come from inside our truck."

"I was wondering about that." Talon motioned toward the parking lot. "I picked up your rental early. I hope that's okay."

"If they gave it to you, that's fine. But we still have to go meet Shadowbox."

Talon chuckled. "Is he still around?"

"He is indeed. And his prices went up too."

"Of course they did." Talon's voice turned grim. "I hear you on that audio recording. There's a part of me that wants to think it's a fake. Did you even consider that?"

"I don't know how they would have done it, but Tesla's hoping the same thing. She's doing an analysis of the tape.

Chances are, we won't find anything for a while. She said it didn't look good. As far as she could tell, it was authentic, at least at this point."

"Shit." Talon shook his head. "Well, I sure as hell didn't do anything to get our asses kicked."

"Neither did we."

"And I can swear there's no way Laszlo would have anything to do with it. He was as loyal as anyone."

"*Was?*" Erick turned to look at him. "Do you know something I don't know?" he asked in alarm.

Talon shook his head. "No, Laszlo is fine. I shouldn't have been speaking in past tense, but I was thinking of back then. I know Laszlo is loyal. He's gone home to his family in Norway for a while. But, if we need him, he's there."

"He doesn't know anything about this though, does he?" Cade asked.

"No, but honestly he approached me over a year ago because he felt somebody had betrayed us too."

"What?" Erick stopped and turned to look at Talon. "You never mentioned that."

"You were just heading under the knife for another major surgery. Cade here had his back half split open and was lying with traction on both legs at the time. Badger was a huge mess. He's had how many surgeries, lost his spleen, his leg... No way I could do that to you guys. Now that you're all back on your feet, and every one of you has the same idea, hell yeah, we need to know. It's all I could do to hold Laszlo back. If he knew we were here, he'd be here."

"Damn."

"It would be nice to see him," Cade said. "Laszlo is a hell of a guy."

Talon led the way to the vehicle. It was an open military

jeep. They dropped their gear in the back, and Talon hopped into the driver's side. "Hotel first?"

"Yeah. Let's give the impression we're here on a holiday."

Cade snorted. "It is a holiday. At least as far as the world is concerned."

"The fewer people who know what we're doing here, the better," Talon said. "Just make sure Badger is keeping track because, if we run into trouble, we will need a fast hand getting out."

"We got that taken care of," Erick said, his voice hard. "Let's go. I want to get this dealt with and get home again."

Both men jumped in and said, "Amen to that."

A few minutes later they pulled up to the hotel. Talon parked in one of the visitor spots. The three men got out and walked into the reception area. Air-conditioning and huge fans blasted them with cool air.

In the waiting area Erick saw a woman on her phone, laptop on her knees, clicking away as she spoke. Obviously Western, she looked impatient and angry.

Cade nudged him with his elbow and motioned toward her. "Don't you know her?"

Talon twisted to look in the same direction as Erick, who stopped and studied her and shook his head. "No, I don't think so."

"Look again," Cade said. "I'm pretty sure she smacked into your '69 Mustang."

At that Erick froze. "She better not have."

"I think it's her."

Erick turned to study her.

She had her hair up, big sunglasses, almost a generic blonde, good looking, slim. Too attractive for over here—it was a dangerous part of the world for white women, particularly if she was traveling alone.

He twisted to look back at his friend. "Why the hell would you think she's the one who did that?"

"Look at her name tag."

His gaze slipped to her chest and caught the name tag he hadn't noticed before. *Honey Lewis.* He froze. "Son of a bitch." His voice was louder than he meant it to be.

Honey glanced at him, and her lips pinched together as she lifted her glasses and stared up at him. Out of her mouth came "What the hell?"

He walked toward her. "Isn't that my line?"

She tapped her foot impatiently on the floor. "I was hoping to never see you again."

"You're the one who smacked into my car."

"It was an accident, remember?"

He nodded. "I remember. I also remember how, at the time, you blamed me."

She raised her hands, palms up. "Sorry, I was upset."

He snorted. "I don't doubt it. At least I got my '69 Mustang fixed. What about you? Are you still driving, or did they yank your license?"

She glared at him. "I still drive, thank you very much." She snapped her laptop closed, stuffed it in a bag, pocketed her cell phone in her khakis and stood. "I shouldn't have been driving that day. You're right. And I apologized. And I shouldn't have blamed you. I wasn't in a very good state of mind."

He punched his hands on his hips. "A year is kinda late for an apology, but I'll accept it."

She gave him a supersweet smile. "Good. It's the only one you'll get." And she spun on her heels and stepped forward to the reception desk, slipping in front of them, taking their place.

He snorted. "Why the hell is she staying here?"

"I don't know, but I like this turn of events," Cade said. "Should make the next few days interesting."

Erick shot him a look. "Like hell." And he stalked forward to speak to a different agent at the counter.

This concludes Book 1 of SEALs of Steel: Badger.
Read about Erick: SEALs of Steel, Book 2

SEALS OF STEEL:
ERICK BOOK 2

When an eight-man unit hit a landmine, all were injured but one died. The remaining seven aim to see his death avenged.

Erick heads to the site of the explosion and his discovery blows him away…

Invited to a conference, Honey runs into Erick, owner of the car she'd smashed into a year ago. She's blindsided by the realization that the man who invited her may not be who she thinks he is.

Book 2 is available now!

To find out more visit Dale Mayer's website.

http://smarturl.it/ErickDale

Author's Note

Thank you for reading Badger: SEALs of Steel, Book 1! If you enjoyed the book, please take a moment and leave a short review.

Dear reader,

I love to hear from readers, and you can contact me at my website: www.dalemayer.com or at my Facebook author page. To be informed of new releases and special offers, sign up for my newsletter or follow me on BookBub. And if you are interested in joining Dale Mayer's Fan Club, here is the Facebook sign up page.
facebook.com/groups/402384989872660

Cheers,
Dale Mayer

Your Free Book Awaits!

KILL OR BE KILLED

Part of an elite SEAL team, Mason takes on the dangerous jobs no one else wants to do – or can do. When he's on a mission, he's focused and dedicated. When he's not, he plays as hard as he fights.

Until he meets a woman he can't have but can't forget. Software developer, Tesla lost her brother in combat and has no intention of getting close to someone else in the military. Determined to save other US soldiers from a similar fate, she's created a program that could save lives. But other countries know about the program, and they won't stop until they get it – and get her.

Time is running out ... For her ... For him ... For them ...

DOWNLOAD a *__complimentary__* copy of MASON? Just tell me where to send it!

http://dalemayer.com/sealsmason/

About the Author

Dale Mayer is a USA Today bestselling author best known for her Psychic Visions and Family Blood Ties series. Her contemporary romances are raw and full of passion and emotion (Second Chances, SKIN), her thrillers will keep you guessing (By Death series), and her romantic comedies will keep you giggling (It's a Dog's Life and Charmin Marvin Romantic Comedy series).

She honors the stories that come to her – and some of them are crazy and break all the rules and cross multiple genres!

To go with her fiction, she also writes nonfiction in many different fields with books available on resume writing, companion gardening and the US mortgage system. She has recently published her Career Essentials Series. All her books are available in print and ebook format.

Connect with Dale Mayer Online

Dale's Website – www.dalemayer.com
Twitter – @DaleMayer
Facebook – facebook.com/DaleMayer.author
BookBub – bookbub.com/authors/dale-mayer

Also by Dale Mayer

Published Adult Books:

Psychic Vision Series
Tuesday's Child
Hide 'n Go Seek
Maddy's Floor
Garden of Sorrow
Knock Knock...
Rare Find
Eyes to the Soul
Now You See Her
Shattered
Into the Abyss
Seeds of Malice
Eye of the Falcon
Itsy-Bitsy Spider
Psychic Visions Books 1–3
Psychic Visions Books 4–6
Psychic Visions Books 7–9

By Death Series
Touched by Death
Haunted by Death
Chilled by Death
By Death Books 1–3

Charmin Marvin Romantic Comedy Series

Broken Protocols
Broken Protocols 2
Broken Protocols 3
Broken Protocols 3.5
Broken Protocols 1-3

Broken and... Mending

Skin
Scars
Scales (of Justice)
Broken but... Mending 1-3

Glory

Genesis
Tori
Celeste
Glory Trilogy

Biker Blues

Biker Blues: Morgan, Part 1
Biker Blues: Morgan, Part 2
Biker Blues: Morgan, Part 3
Biker Baby Blues: Morgan, Part 4
Biker Blues: Morgan, Full Set
Biker Blues: Salvation, Part 1
Biker Blues: Salvation, Part 2
Biker Blues: Salvation, Part 3
Biker Blues: Salvation, Full Set

SEALs of Honor

Mason: SEALs of Honor, Book 1

Hawk: SEALs of Honor, Book 2
Dane: SEALs of Honor, Book 3
Swede: SEALs of Honor, Book 4
Shadow: SEALs of Honor, Book 5
Cooper: SEALs of Honor, Book 6
Markus: SEALs of Honor, Book 7
Evan: SEALs of Honor, Book 8
Mason's Wish: SEALs of Honor, Book 9
Chase: SEALs of Honor, Book 10
Brett: SEALs of Honor, Book 11
Devlin: SEALs of Honor, Book 12
Easton: SEALs of Honor, Book 13
Ryder: SEALs of Honor, Book 14
Macklin: SEALs of Honor, Book 15
Corey: SEALs of Honor, Book 16
Warrick: SEALs of Honor, Book 17
SEALs of Honor, Books 1–3
SEALs of Honor, Books 4–6
SEALs of Honor, Books 7–10
SEALs of Honor, Books 11–13

Heroes for Hire

Levi's Legend: Heroes for Hire, Book 1
Stone's Surrender: Heroes for Hire, Book 2
Merk's Mistake: Heroes for Hire, Book 3
Rhodes's Reward: Heroes for Hire, Book 4
Flynn's Firecracker: Heroes for Hire, Book 5
Logan's Light: Heroes for Hire, Book 6
Harrison's Heart: Heroes for Hire, Book 7
Saul's Sweetheart: Heroes for Hire, Book 8
Dakota's Delight: Heroes for Hire, Book 9
Tyson's Treasure: Heroes for Hire, Book 10

Jace's Jewel: Heroes for Hire, Book 11
Rory's Rose: Heroes for Hire, Book 12
Brandon's Bliss: Heroes for Hire, Book 13
Liam's Lily: Heroes for Hire, Book 14
Heroes for Hire, Books 1–3
Heroes for Hire, Books 4–6
Heroes for Hire, Books 7–9

SEALs of Steel
Badger: SEALs of Steel, Book 1
Erick: SEALs of Steel, Book 2

Collections
Dare to Be You…
Dare to Love…
Dare to be Strong…
RomanceX3

Standalone Novellas
It's a Dog's Life
Riana's Revenge
Second Chances

Published Young Adult Books:

Family Blood Ties Series
Vampire in Denial
Vampire in Distress
Vampire in Design
Vampire in Deceit
Vampire in Defiance
Vampire in Conflict

Vampire in Chaos
Vampire in Crisis
Vampire in Control
Vampire in Charge
Family Blood Ties Set 1–3
Family Blood Ties Set 1–5
Family Blood Ties Set 4–6
Family Blood Ties Set 7–9
Sian's Solution, A Family Blood Ties Series Prequel
    Novelette

Design series
Dangerous Designs
Deadly Designs
Darkest Designs
Design Series Trilogy

Standalone
In Cassie's Corner
Gem Stone (a Gemma Stone Mystery)
Time Thieves

Published Non-Fiction Books:

Career Essentials
Career Essentials: The Résumé
Career Essentials: The Cover Letter
Career Essentials: The Interview
Career Essentials: 3 in 1

CPSIA information can be obtained
at www.ICGtesting.com
Printed in the USA
BVHW03s0723130518
516102BV00017B/707/P